W9-CDW-736

6501040

realistic fiction

DATE DUE

FEB 7 2017		
FEB 2 3 2017		
APR 3 2017		
APR 1 1 2017		
DEC 2 8 2017		
JAN 3 2018		
SEP 1 4 2018		
SEP 2 8 2018		
12/17		
2/1		
12/17/19		
1/23/20		
9/14/20		
9/30/21		

PERMA-BOUND

SKINNY

DONNA COONER

Point

No part of this publication may be reproduced, stored in a retrieval system, or transmitted in any form or by any means, electronic, mechanical, photocopying, recording, or otherwise, without written permission of the publisher. For information regarding permission, write to Scholastic Inc., Attention: Permissions Department, 557 Broadway, New York, NY 10012.

All rights reserved. Published by Point, an imprint of Scholastic Inc. SCHOLASTIC, POINT, and associated logos are trademarks and/or registered trademarks of Scholastic Inc.

This book was originally published in hardcover by Point in 2012.

ISBN 978-0-545-42764-7

Copyright © 2012 by Donna Cooner

12 11 10 9 8 7 6 5 4 3   14 15 16 17 18 19/0

Printed in the U.S.A.   40
This edition first printing, April 2014

Book design by Elizabeth B. Parisi

FOR MY SISTER, MARTY, WHO JUST
WANTED ME TO STOP READING
AND GO OUTSIDE TO PLAY.

ASHES

CHAPTER ONE

know what they think because she whispers their thoughts into my ear. I can hear them. Clearly. Constantly.

"If I ever look like that, just kill me."

Her name is Skinny.

I don't know how long she's been sitting there on my shoulder, whispering her messages. She popped up when I was about ten, when I started gaining weight after my mother died. At first, her voice came infrequently . . . softly . . . but as I got bigger, she grew stronger. She probably looks like a goth Tinker Bell, maybe a winged fairy kind of thing, but I've never actually seen her. I only hear her.

I squeeze down the aisle of my sophomore algebra class to the far back corner accompanied by the swishing sound of my thighs rubbing together with each step.

"You're huge."

Skinny whispers in my ear the thoughts of size-zero

Whitney Stone as I push by her desk, almost knocking her purse off in the process. Whitney gives a big sigh of disgust, rolls her eyes, and moves the knockoff Prada to the other side of the desk.

Believe me, Whitney. I wouldn't come near you if I didn't have to, but I can't escape it. I can't escape me. Trapped in layers of blubber and excess everything. It all feels tight . . . stretched . . . uncomfortable. From the moment I wake up in the morning and struggle to stand up out of my bed to the moment I go to sleep at night, I am trapped inside this enormous shell. The anger I keep stuffed beneath the layers seeps out toward Whitney, an easy target.

"So, Whitney, my sister said you did really well on cheerleader tryouts. You know, all except for that one part . . ." I let my voice trail off and wait for the fear to take over her eyes. Small satisfaction. I feel a pang of guilt and push the anger back down inside.

"What is she talking about?" I hear Whitney ask behind me as I move on.

She has no idea that my older stepsister, Lindsey, head cheerleader for Huntsville High School, hasn't spoken a word to me in weeks. Lindsey's not mad at me. I'm just not worthy of conversation. But Whitney doesn't know that. She turns to confront her clueless best friend and fellow cheerleader-wannabe, Kristen Rogers. "You said it was perfect."

"Good one." Gigi Retodo, drama geek, smiles broadly at my comment. As I waddle on down the aisle, she slaps me a high five as though we're friends. We're not. I think she just dislikes me a little less than she does Whitney. Evidently "fat" wins over "popular" with the thespians.

"You're like the big marshmallow monster in that old Ghostbusters *movie. Soft. Gooey. Horrifying,"* Skinny says softly in my left ear.

I push on down the aisle because I don't really have a choice. I pass Jackson Barnett on my right. He wears jeans with a blue tee under an unbuttoned long-sleeved plaid shirt. I notice the three leather loops around his right wrist as he reaches up to push his dark hair out of his eyes. His style is meticulously thought-out to look deceptively unplanned. I love that about him, but then I love everything about him. If only I could touch him. I'd burrow into his side and wrap my arms around his flat stomach, stretching up on my tiptoes to lay my head on his broad shoulder. And I know exactly how that would feel because I've been right there. Once upon a time.

I wait for Skinny to whisper Jackson's thoughts in my ear, but nothing comes.

I don't know what's worse. The fact that Jackson doesn't think bad things about me, or the fact that he doesn't think about me at all. When he was scrawny with buckteeth and glasses, he used to think about me all the time. Now that he's tall, with straight white teeth and contacts, he's forgotten the tree house we made in his backyard and kissing me behind the street sign on Gardenia Street. As I covered myself in grief and fat over the years, his memory of me as his best friend trickled away until now I am completely unrecognizable. I know the feeling. I don't recognize me, either.

Jackson turns to laugh at something Whitney says about a party last weekend. I push on. Look ahead. Anticipate space available. The back row always fills up first, but I'm usually here early enough to snag a seat. Not today. Scan the room. Is there space for me? Somewhere? Only two desks are available. Both are the kind with the desktop that snaps down over your stomach. Only it won't snap down over my stomach. I'll leave the desk up, but then I'll have to balance my notebook and books in my lap. A lap that really doesn't exist.

"You'll drop things. Things you won't be able to pick up. People will stare and giggle and point. You will be noticed. Do you really want that?"

I look around the room once more. No other choice. I slide into one of the chairs, my bottom falling over both sides of the seat. I put my book bag on the floor beside me and carefully hook the strap over one arm. Don't let it fall. If it falls then everything will be out of my reach for the rest of class. I pull the strap up until I can manage to reach inside. Rummaging around, I look for a pen and notebook. Pulling them out, I try not to make much noise. I don't want anyone's attention. I rest the notebook awkwardly on my stomach and try to turn to today's blank page. Finally, I'm ready. Everything is hard.

The teacher looks toward me.

"Look at the pity in his eyes."

I guess that's better than the disdain I see in most of the teachers' eyes and the outright fear I see from most other kids. Fear that it could happen to them.

"Look. She can't even fit in the chair."

Skinny doesn't have to whisper that in my ear. I can hear it plainly. Kristen Rogers doesn't even lower her voice. She is wearing a little pink tank top with the glittery word "Juicy" across the boobs. People think being fat somehow affects your hearing.

"I didn't know pants came in that size," Kristen says. "Maybe I should go on a diet. I told you my jeans were getting tight."

"Don't worry. You'll never look like that," her petite best friend Whitney responds. I know she's right. Neither one of them will ever look like me. I don't know why, but I know it's true.

"Gigi Retodo has an announcement to make before class starts." Mr. Blair waves Gigi up to the front of the room. "Only five minutes," he warns.

Gigi's face is an exotic combination of her Filipino father and Texan mother — creamy olive skin and almost black, almond-shaped eyes. But the bright blue bangs and the pink hair that fades into purple around the back of her neck distract from the pretty face. They're definitely what you notice first. Today she's wearing red leggings and sparkly high-top tennis shoes. She's tiny, with elf-like features and the body of a twelve-year-old boy. It's March, but she still has a purple-striped scarf wrapped around her neck. She moves with a jittery grace that makes me think she just ate a sackful of candy and is dancing it off.

"The drama club wants to invite all of you to the spring musical in April," Gigi says in a surprisingly big voice for such a little person. Then with an amazing lack of self-consciousness, she bursts into song. "*Oooooooo . . . klahoma . . .*"

She dances around the front of the room, like Rainbow Brite on speed. Her voice is strong and on pitch even without accompaniment. It's a good voice, but I can sing better. A secret no one in this room knows.

"But who wants to see an elephant dancing around?"

Everyone bursts into applause at Gigi's final, flourishing bow. I glance over at Jackson. His teeth are flashing in a blazing smile as he claps enthusiastically. There used to be braces on those teeth. I remember. Mr. Blair gets the class back on track, and I try to concentrate on algebra. Skinny is quiet at my ear. Good. If I stay very still, maybe I can stop the whispering.

Chance Lehmann, his rich ebony hair curling wildly out from underneath the New York Yankees baseball cap he has pulled low over his eyes, slides into the chair across from me. He's ten minutes late. Early for him. I shake my head at him when he meets my eyes, but one side of my mouth creeps up in a half smile. Chance has that effect on people. His mouth twists down in a grimace, his puppy-dog brown eyes fake sad, and then he waves a hand briefly in hello. His skin is a dark honey color. The better to notice the sparkling purple fingernail polish on his hands.

"You like?" He holds his hands out toward me, palms down. "It's called Jammin' Jelly."

I look to see if Mr. Blair is paying attention, but he's talking to someone in the front row about their homework. "Do your toes match?" I whisper across the aisle.

"Of course. I'm completely in touch with my feminine side." Chance grins at me, fanning his face with one purple-painted hand. That might be true, but he's also "completely in touch" with a baseball and can pitch an amazing curveball that will buy his way into any university he wants to attend, painted toenails and all. "You should try it, Ever. A mani/pedi is exactly what you need."

"You can paint a pig, but it's still a pig," Skinny whispers in my ear.

I frown at Chance and turn toward the front of the room again. Mr. Blair calls a couple of students to the board to work on some problems. Panic rises in my chest. *Don'tcallonme. Don'tcallonme.* The idea of squeezing through the aisle to display my backside to the whole room's comments makes me start to breathe hard.

"Ever Davies," the teacher calls out. "Will you tackle problem number seventeen?"

It isn't a request. I'm trapped. Inside and outside my body. I push my way out of the chair, which clings to me like a big inner tube, and start back up the aisle.

Kristen Rogers rolls her eyes at Whitney.

"Oh my god. Here you come again," Skinny jeers.

I'm fifteen years old, and I weigh 302 pounds.

CHAPTER TWO

E ver!"

I look for the voice calling my name, but the crowd leaving school is always so chaotic. Students rush out every doorway to the outside — squealing, yelling, and laughing. Groups of kids huddle together outside in clumps, even though it has started to rain. There is a blue tint to the sky off in the distance.

I walk toward the street and pass a group of boys. One shoves the other in the chest and yells "Jerk!" The other screams "Shut up!" and the pushing match is on. The other boys just laugh and I make a wide circle around them to avoid the possibility of being an unintended casualty.

Three grime-covered school buses pull up to the curb. I step sideways to avoid the black, smelly exhaust pouring from the tailpipe of the first one in line. Most of the windows are already occupied with tired, blank-looking faces. At least I don't have to ride the bus home anymore. Dodging a boy carrying a trombone case, I practically flatten a girl picking up scattered papers from the front drive. Finally, I see Rat in his beat-up Honda Civic across the circle drive, waving frantically. I weave through the masses and wait at the curb as a red truck full of junior boys goes by.

"Congrats on getting the outstanding sophomore writing award." It's Kevin Somethingorother, a tall, pale kid with bad acne who sits near the back wall in our third-period English class.

"Ummm . . . thanks." I smile at him, feeling a little guilty that I never really noticed him much before and that I can't remember his last name. The compliment makes me uncomfortable. "I'm not too sure about this whole award assembly thing. Giving them out in March seems a bit premature. I still have plenty of time to screw something up, right?"

"You won't have to do anything. Just smile and wave when your name is called."

I nod as though winning awards is pretty normal for me.

Make fun of yourself. It makes them feel more comfortable, Skinny says.

"No problem. I have plenty of practice doing that from my beauty-pageant days." I give a cheesy beauty queen wave, and he laughs. It feels good to make someone else smile.

"You're a pretty good writer yourself," I say. He looks pleased, and I search my memory to say something kind to keep the smile on his face. "Your essay on global warming last week was one of the best in the class. Making nonfiction interesting is always a challenge."

"Thanks," Kevin says, "but yours was *the* best in the class. Hands down. Brilliant idea to turn the scientific method into a musical. Who couldn't sing along with 'Hypothesis Dreams'? I don't know how you come up with this stuff."

"Thanks," I say, feeling a proud flush on my cheeks.

The red truck full of boys slows at the curb. A guy leans out the passenger window and yells at me, "Hey, tons of fun!"

They drive past slowly, the rest of the boys inside laughing hysterically. I try to pretend I don't hear it. It's *not* okay to drive around the high school parking lot and yell out at people, "You read like a third grader" or "Your dad's a drunk," but for some reason all the groups unite to comment about my weight.

"The world doesn't care if you're kind and good. It only cares that you're fat. Nothing else matters."

"My ride is waiting," I say to Kevin. We both ignore the boys like it didn't even happen.

"See you tomorrow," he says, but the smile is gone.

I negotiate the traffic in the driveway and pull open the passenger door of Rat's car.

"You're late," Rat says. I squeeze into the front seat, ignoring the seat belt. We both know it doesn't fit.

"Sorry."

Carefully, he pulls out into the traffic but immediately has to stop for a group of four senior cheerleaders. They all wear their tiny green miniskirts and tight Hornet tank tops that don't quite reach the waists of their skirts. Shoulders back, hair streaming behind, they walk with the confidence of beauty. I watch the line of their naked flat stomachs strut across the street to catcalls and whistles. For the millionth time today I wonder what it might feel like to walk like that for just a day . . . an hour . . . a minute.

"Ugly Number One's looking good." Rat watches their giggling parade with a focus that makes me remember he's a sixteen-year-old boy. He's talking about my oldest stepsister, Lindsey, who strides along in the middle of the line of prancing cheerleaders.

Rat's real name is Theodore Simon Wilson but only stubborn English teachers call him that now. Most everyone else calls him the nickname bestowed upon him by mean little third-graders who saw the likeness between his long-nosed face and the drawings of the rat in *Charlotte's Web*. It stuck long after he grew into his face and tall, lanky body. I once asked him if he'd rather me call him Theodore or Teddy or Ted, but he just blinked at me from behind his glasses and asked, "Why?"

"Your stepmother know about the new belly button piercing?" Rat asks me. Evidently, we both saw the new bling dangling from Lindsey's stomach.

Lindsey glances toward the car, and her eyes meet mine for a brief second. There is a shock of recognition. I give her a five-fingered wave. I know it will piss her off. She looks away and keeps walking.

"You embarrass her," Skinny whispers. Like I didn't know that.

"They don't know you're alive," I mutter. I say it to Rat, but I know it's true for me, too.

"Somebody's in a good mood."

Rat is brilliant in a "build your own optical resonator laser in your backyard, start a small grass fire, and get community service" kind of way. He's not brilliant in the "get a date with a cheerleader" kind of way. We both know it. I didn't have to say it. I turn to stare out the passenger-side window.

"Where's Cerissa?" I ask. One of the Fabulous Five, senior cheerleader Cerissa Stevens, is missing.

"She was expelled last week for urinating in the soft drink she served her ex-boyfriend at the basketball game," Rat says.

"Gimme a *P*!" I say, shaking fake pom-poms in the air.

At the end of the driveway, Gigi Retodo and two other drama geeks wave a big cardboard sign announcing the upcoming musical. Gigi's changed into a pioneer-era costume, which looks really bizarre with her blue/pink/purple hair. Standing on tiptoes, she belts out the title song while the two boys run around frantically trying to get kids to take their flyers.

Jackson stands at the corner watching Gigi. Just seeing the look on his face, I feel a sharp jab of jealousy kick into my stomach. My throat aches with the desire to have him look at me like that. I would do anything. I blink to clear the longing out of my eyes before Rat sees.

Rat glances over at me. I'm not quick enough.

"Did you say something about someone not knowing you're alive?" Rat's voice is dry. I ignore him. Rat knows how I feel about Jackson. He was, after all, Jackson's delivery boy for that note so long ago that read, "Do you like me? Circle yes or no."

A tall boy that I vaguely recognize from American history class punches Jackson once in the arm, distracting him from Gigi, and they scuffle across the median, laughing and yelling. I'm not close enough to see the crinkles around Jackson's dark blue-green eyes, but I know they're there. He used to laugh with me like that. About 150 pounds ago.

"They're doing *Oklahoma* for the spring musical," I say to Rat.

"I saw. Why don't you try out?"

Rat pushes his glasses up over the slight bump on his nose. He got it when he broke his nose playing kickball at recess in the second grade. I know because I was the one who kicked the ball. That tiny mark under his left eye is from my lightsaber at his fifth birthday party. I also know he has a jagged scar on his left calf from when we were eight and jumped off the pier into Lake Conroe. We were holding hands and he said, "Jump," and I said, "Wait." That was also the year Jackson Barnett moved in down the street and, for a short time, two best friends became Three Musketeers.

"Maybe next year," I say. "They do a musical every spring. Besides *Oklahoma*'s never really been one of my favorites."

"Right."

We both know I won't be trying out this spring or next spring or any spring after that. It doesn't matter that I have the best voice in the school. It just matters that there aren't many parts for a 300-pound girl who just wants to be invisible.

Rat turns left out of the school parking lot. He's been my personal driver since he got his license six months ago. It means

Lindsey doesn't have to know me anymore, which works for Lindsey. It also means I now have to go wherever Rat goes after school and that includes community service.

We pass the Walmart on the right and then McKenzie's BarBQ on the left. It doesn't take long to get anywhere in this town. An hour north of Houston, Huntsville sits on the edge of the East Texas Piney Woods and has some odd extremes when it comes to attractions. Visitors can go to the Texas Prison Museum and see "Old Sparky," the electric chair that killed 361 condemned criminals over forty years of service, or head south of town to view the world's tallest statue of an American hero — Sam Houston. Rat's dad is a ranger for Sam Houston Park. His mom, an elementary school teacher, was my mom's best friend from the moment we moved in next door to them. I still see the grief in Mrs. Wilson's eyes when she looks at me.

I glance over at Rat. "Your hands are blue," I say. I'm not really surprised.

"One hand. The left," he says, "and it's indigo."

"Why?" I ask.

"I was synthesizing one of eighteen azo dyes according to a parallel combinatorial synthesis scheme."

"Uh-huh," I say, really sorry I asked.

"After the exothermic reaction subsided, I collected the precipitated indigo by suction filtration."

I know from experience this can go on forever. "And you spilled it on your hand," I interrupt quickly.

"There were several more steps before that occurred." Rat sighs in frustration at the idea of a good chemistry experiment story cut short, but he finally admits, "But, yes, that was the eventual outcome."

We pass Tinsley's Fried Chicken with the big sign outside that reads, TRY OUR BIG, JUICY BREASTS.

"They really should change that sign," I say.

"Why?" Rat asks. He slows at the corner, his indigo hand spinning the wheel into the right turn, and changes the subject.

"Ugly Number Two has homework tonight," Rat says. "A poem written from the perspective of one of the characters in *Huckleberry Finn*."

"It will cost her," I mumble. Briella, my other stepsister, is a sophomore like me and Rat, and she's in his sixth-period English class.

"I'm thinking maybe *Dreamgirls* download?" Rat says. I nod. "Original cast or movie?"

"I already have the original cast. Movie."

"She needs it by Wednesday."

"She'll get it tomorrow if she can pay."

Briella gets a hefty allowance from her real father every week in child support. Most of it goes toward clothes and shoes, but a growing percentage comes my way these days. I work for iTunes downloads and guarantee at least a B. I also agree to never take the credit for her passable creative writing. It seems to work for both of us.

"Can't you just drop me off at home before you go to the center?" I ask.

"We're already late. Besides, a little community service never hurt anybody."

I always ask. He always says no. I sigh, but the truth is I don't really mind. The age-five-and-under kids at the Sam Houston Boys and Girls Club are probably the only people in the world who might actually miss me if I didn't show up. Anyway, I like to think so.

We enter the building and part ways. Rat goes toward the office. He's doing something with their computer database. I don't ask many questions.

I head toward the door in the back where the youngest kids hang out. Skinny takes a break. Weird thing about hanging out with five-year-olds: You don't need anyone to tell you what they're thinking. They just say it right out loud.

Like the first time I came with Rat to the center. A little dark-eyed boy came and stood in front of me while I waited in the hallway.

"You're really, really fat," he said.

"I know," I said.

He sat down in the chair next to me, sliding back into the seat until his feet dangled above the floor. Kicking his feet slowly back and forth, we sat in silence for a few minutes.

"My name is Mario. What's yours?"

"Ever."

"Like happily ever after?"

"Yes."

Leaning into my shoulder, he looked up at my face intently.

"Do you know any stories?"

"Yes."

"Good." Sliding out of the chair, he took my hand and tugged me back to the playroom. And that was that. I've been coming here and telling stories ever since.

Today there's a big commotion when I enter the playroom. I'm noticed, and not in a bad way. Instantly, tiny hands pull at me, touch me, reach for me. I don't flinch or jerk away.

"You're *finally* here." Valerie Ramirez, the tiny five-year-old drama queen, rolls her eyes. "Do you know how long we've been *waiting*?"

"A long time," Mario says solemnly. He's always so serious.

"How's kindergarten?" I hope the change of subject will help me get out of the doghouse.

"School's a lot of work," Mario says.

I laugh. "You've got a long way to go. What's your favorite part?"

"I liked the letter *C*."

"More than the letter *A*?" I ask, smiling.

"*A* was boring. We had to eat apples."

"And what did you eat for the letter *C*?"

"Chocolate candy." He grins. I grin back.

"We sing a lot in kindergarten. I like that."

"I liked that part of kindergarten, too," I say.

Valerie clutches her best friend Keisha's hand and swings it, making all the brightly clipped pigtails on Keisha's head fly about wildly.

"Ever, it's *story* time!" Valerie proclaims. Keisha nods furiously and giggles.

"*Cinderella. Cinderella,*" they chant like the mice in the Disney movie version.

I settle into a special setup of three wooden chairs, which they have already lined up to hold me. And I begin.

"Once upon a time there was a girl named Cinderella," I say.

"No!" they scream in anguish. "Sing it!"

I know the lyrics by heart. Just like I know almost all the lyrics to any musical by heart. It's a well-guarded secret that only a select group of poor five-year-olds have somehow coaxed out of me. I sang *Cats* last week and bits of *Wicked* the week before, but they always come back to their favorite, *Cinderella*.

But I don't sing. Not yet. If there's anything I've learned about telling stories to kids, it's to keep them in suspense.

Mario says he'll be the prince, but only if he can be the Phantom next time. The two girls agree, and the three of them dance across the block-strewn carpet with gusto.

"Tell me the part about the prince again." Keisha pulls away from the rest of the group and pushes her way into my lap, snuggling in like my body is some kind of floppy blanket. She's still breathing hard from the dancing, her tiny pink T-shirt moving rhythmically up and down over her chest.

Mario stops to make a flourishing bow in front of Valerie. Keisha leans back against my chest to pop a thumb into her mouth as I speak.

"And they danced and danced until the clock struck midnight," I say, as Mario and Valerie waltz wildly among the scattered blocks.

"And they were happy?" Keisha asks.

"They were happier than they'd ever been in their whole life," I say. For some reason the words bring tears to my eyes. I don't know why. It isn't a sad story.

The dancing five-year-olds end up in a giggling pile of bodies in the middle of the home center.

"*Now* sing," Mario commands. But I don't because Valerie jumps up suddenly, grabbing between her legs.

"I gots to use it!" she declares and gallops toward the bathroom.

It's hard to argue with that. Cinderella's ball stops.

I see Rat standing in the doorway, tall and serious, watching me. He shifts uncomfortably from one foot to the other. I'm not sure how long he's been there.

"I have to go," I tell the kids.

"Nooooo," they squeal, grabbing my arms and begging me to stay. Valerie returns to join in the begging.

"Just one song," she pleads, stamping her tiny tennis shoe on the red ABC carpet for emphasis.

"Sorry. My ride is here."

"You mean your carriage?" Mario asks with a rare smile.

I look up at Rat and grin. He smiles back and pushes his glasses up on his nose.

"*He thinks you look ridiculous.*" Skinny is back. Lately, she's started to do Rat. I don't like it.

"Let's go." I push past him, the smile gone from my face.

CHAPTER THREE

My stepsister Briella is already at the kitchen table when I walk in the door. Meat loaf and mashed potatoes sit untouched on the plate in front of her while she texts frantically in her lap.

"Eat your dinner, Briella," my stepmother, Charlotte, says from the kitchen.

My mom, my real mom, was an artist. She illustrated children's books. Fairy tales, picture books, animals. She was amazing. Sometimes I would fall in love with one of the illustrations, and she would give it to me. I kept them in her old portfolio in my closet. Bears with clothes on, kids going to school, but the one I kept on my wall — my very favorite — was an illustration of Beauty dancing with the Beast. She painted that one when she was pregnant with me.

"I told you no gravy," Briella says, not looking up from her phone. She's wearing a black pleated miniskirt and a soft, bright blue sweater that hugs her fifteen-year-old curves. I know without looking under the table that she's also wearing black Ugg boots. The miniskirt and the sweater I covet, but those black fur-lined boots with all that room left around her tiny calves make me absolutely livid.

I'm starving. All I had to eat today for lunch was a salad and an orange. Of course that didn't include the three Snickers I stuffed down one after another in the bathroom stall between fifth and sixth periods, or the Little Debbie Honey Buns I bought from the vending machine when I was supposed to be at the library. I try to hide the actual eating part from almost everyone, especially the bad stuff that I'm not supposed to eat, because everyone knows the fat girl is going to devour the big chocolate sundae with the sprinkles on top, right? It's expected. Publicly, at the school lunchroom table, I eat salads and fruit. But secretively I continually push enough food into my body to result in my current weight. That's a lot of secrets to swallow.

It's harder to keep the pretense up at home. I pick up a blueberry muffin off the countertop and cram a quick bite in while I look for the plate in the pantry. Charlotte frowns at me. I know what she's thinking just by her glance.

"Do you really need that muffin, too? You're going to eat dinner," Skinny hisses.

Charlotte isn't a bad person, and she obviously loves my dad. She just isn't my mom. Her blond hair is perfectly cut into a smooth bob of highlighted strands. Hair spray, a straightening iron, mousse, gel, and *lots* of time are required to get to this final look. She also never leaves the house without makeup. It's a rule. My mom's idea of makeup was the tiny bit of shiny clear lip gloss she put on before she left for the store.

It's different now.

"Is Dad here?" I ask.

"He's going to be late. Go ahead and eat without him," Charlotte says. She rinses off a spoon in the sink and opens up the dishwasher to stick it inside. "I'll keep it warm and eat with him when he gets here."

Not a big surprise. Dad works late a lot. He's a Walker County Sheriff, and he's been pretty busy lately. Last week, Bubba Rose pleaded guilty to attempted felony theft after Dad caught him stuffing a lead weight in a fish during a tournament at Lake Conroe in an attempt to win the grand prize, a fifty-five-thousand-dollar fishing boat. What can I say? Fishing is serious here in Texas. The week before that Dad helped catch an escaped prisoner who had broken out more than seventy times to go shop across the street at the Walmart.

I push the rest of the muffin into my mouth, crumbs dribbling down my shirt, and carry a fully loaded plate of meat loaf, mashed potatoes, and gravy over to the table. I sit down next to Briella. She glances over at me, looking pointedly at the food on my plate. I know what she's thinking, too. I know what everyone is thinking about me. All I have to do is listen to the voice in my ear.

"How can anyone possibly eat all that? And you wonder why you are huge?"

I take an enormous bite of mashed potatoes and gravy, looking directly at my stepsister. She rolls her eyes at me.

"Where's Lindsey?" Charlotte asks.

"I don't know," I mumble around a huge bite, the gravy dripping down my chin. But even though I just walked in the door, I do know. Everyone knows. She's in front of the mirror in her room, applying a final coat of mascara or lip gloss or hair gel. As head cheerleader, she's like God. And no one disturbs God on the evening of the Friday pep rally. Especially when it's the night before the basketball playoff game.

I break off a piece of meat loaf with my fingers and slide it under the table. It's snatched from my hand.

"Ever, do not feed that goat from the table," Charlotte says. She is referring to Roxanne, our chocolate Lab puppy. The goat dog, as Charlotte prefers to call her, is in trouble because she got into the pantry yesterday and ate two kiwis, a raw potato, and most of a pound of sugar. The rest of the sugar was scattered across the kitchen floor in a fine layer of gritty carpet that we'll still be feeling weeks from now. Roxanne also chewed up a hardback book from Charlotte's library, ate her fur headband, and put holes in her black tights. I didn't tell Charlotte I'd also seen Roxanne standing on the dining-room table last week, licking the wooden top. Roxanne and I have to stick together. Neither one of us is on Charlotte's list of favorite things.

Charlotte frowns down at her coffee cup as she refills it at the kitchen counter. No matter what time of the day it is,

Charlotte usually has a cup of coffee in her perfectly manicured hand.

"She hates you," Skinny says. *"She wishes you weren't here."*

I finish up the mashed potatoes and take a bite of the meat loaf. Briella is still texting, her food sitting untouched on the table.

"Have you done your homework?" Charlotte asks. I know she's not asking me, so I ignore her.

Briella makes a noise that's supposed to sound like a yes but can later be said to be a no. I glance her way, but she doesn't raise her eyes from the phone in her lap. It doesn't matter. Based on Rat's information about her English assignment, she'll be looking for me soon enough.

"Your dad sent the check today," Charlotte says.

Briella looks up from the phone in her lap.

"Did he say anything about this weekend?" she asks. "Is he coming?"

"He didn't say, but I wouldn't count on it, Briella. He's really busy these days."

"Right," Briella says, and goes back to texting. Roxanne licks my hand to remind me she's still under the table. Waiting.

"You're invisible to everyone but the dog," Skinny says.

I clean my plate, then walk over to the dishwasher to put my dishes inside. Charlotte moves over to let me pass. A car honks outside and Charlotte walks over to the front window, pulls back the shades, and peers outside.

"Lindsey!" Charlotte turns away from the window to yell up the stairs. "You're going to be late. Hannah is here."

No answer from upstairs.

Roxanne follows me, looking up with her big, golden "I'm starving to death down here" eyes. When Charlotte looks away, I slide a piece of meat loaf into a napkin and then into my pocket. Roxanne wags her tail just a little bit and goes to wait for me at the bottom of the stairs. She might be part goat, but she's not stupid.

"I'm going to do my homework," I say to nobody, picking up my backpack from the couch and pulling myself up the stairs. Roxanne matches my slow pace, step for step, sniffing at my pocket. Halfway up, we are both confronted with the whirlwind of perfume and pom-poms that is Lindsey. Her dark, almost black, hair is pulled into a perky ponytail and tied with a ribbon in the green-and-gold school colors. The short, pleated cheerleading skirt flounces around her tan thighs as she jogs down the stairs in perfectly matching tennis shoes. Roxanne and I both squeeze to one side of the staircase to let her size-two body pass as she rushes for the door, leaving glittery strands of green plastic behind.

"Hey," she says to Charlotte and Briella, and then she's gone with a door slam.

Roxanne and I keep going up the stairs and into my room at the end of the hall. The meat loaf is gobbled up from the napkin almost before I can shut the bedroom door behind us.

"You're welcome," I say to Roxanne. She wags her tail, jumps up on the end of my bed, and settles into a big circle of soft brown fur with a huge sigh of satisfaction. I pull out my iPod and push the earbuds into my ears. Turning up the volume, I dig around for an algebra book in the bottom of my backpack. I get to the right page of the assignment, which I carefully wrote in my homework folder, take out a properly sharpened pencil, write my name at the top of the blank page and then . . . I close my eyes and lean back against my headboard. The music is what I want, not algebra. I need the melody, the harmony, the emotion of the music. My mind takes flight behind my closed eyes.

Then suddenly, the earbuds are yanked out. Briella. I'd been expecting her, but the sudden interruption of Kristin Chenoweth's original cast version of "Popular" is a rude awakening. Roxanne jumps down off the bed and finds a spot out of sight under my desk. Even the dog feels the wintry gust of air that always seems to accompany my younger stepsister.

Briella stands just inside the bedroom door, hands on her impossibly tiny hips, glaring at me with icy blue eyes. The exact opposite in coloring to her dark older sister, she inherited all the genes from her mother's German ancestors while Lindsey looks just like her father's Portuguese side of the family. She's dressed for bed in some tiny green sleeping shorts and a tank top; her long, thin legs are bare. With her strawberry hair combed into long, loose pigtails, Briella's face is free of any makeup. A rare sight to see. She looks impossibly gorgeous.

"You could have knocked." I push over to the side of my bed and confront her.

"I did. You were playing that stupid music so loud you didn't hear me."

"I wouldn't call it stupid if I were you. Not if you want that poem on Huck Finn."

"You heard," she mumbles. "Nerdy rat boy."

"That's going to cost you. The price just went up to two downloads."

"Come on, Ever," she whines. "I don't have that much this week. I need a new dress for the homecoming dance on Friday."

"But you also need a poem by Thursday." I smile up at her. "It's a dilemma."

"Fine," she snaps. "Use my password. You know it."

I shove my body back up to the headboard and lean back in triumph. The bed creaks. I start to push the earbuds back into my ears, but she isn't leaving. She looks down at me with a sneer.

"How does that bed hold up under all your weight?"

"What?" I ask.

"You don't have to always act like that."

"Like what?"

"Like you're better than everyone else. Like you're smarter and . . ." She pauses, searching for the right word, then spits it out, "special."

"Yeah, I'm special all right," I mumble sarcastically, thinking how ironic it is that I was telling the five-year-olds the tale of Cinderella earlier. "I'm the poor, motherless stepsister that does all the work around here."

My mom was like me. It was obvious to everyone we had the same genes — the same rounded, curvy, pear-shaped bodies of *her* mother and two sisters. She was always on a diet. One time it was the cabbage soup diet that made the whole house smell for weeks. Another time it was strawberry protein shakes that tasted like ground-up oatmeal. By the time I was nine, I was on a diet, too. Not because I was fat, because according to the pictures of me I was a pretty normal-sized little girl. But I guess my mom could see my future. So we joined Weight Watchers together — the only mother/daughter team.

Then came the exercise craze. We walked, we Jazzercised, we did water aerobics. We balanced encyclopedias on our ankles, holding up our legs inches off the living room carpet until we couldn't stand the burning thigh muscles any longer.

"Give me a break. Poor Ever. I got it. Your mom's gone," Briella says. "But at least she's dead."

"What are you talking about?" How dare she talk about my mother? Briella didn't know anything about her. She didn't know the one constant in the midst of all the dieting and exercise was the Snickers we ate in the car on the way home from the grocery store so my dad wouldn't see that once again we had fallen off the wagon. My mom's laughter and chocolate — forever connected. For months, maybe even years, I ate chocolate before bedtime thinking it would help me dream about her and she wouldn't be gone. In my little kid brain it seemed to work, until I woke up the next morning and remembered the loss all over again. The dreams stopped, but the nightly chocolate ritual continued. It still goes on today.

Briella didn't know that in the end none of it mattered. The chemo made my mom so sick she didn't want to eat anything, not even the candy bars I would sneak into her hospital room. Cancer was the ultimate diet.

Nobody knew all that but me.

"She can't come back," Briella says. Like I haven't thought that every single day since she's been gone? "No matter how much she wants to, and she would want to. She would have never chosen to leave you."

"What's your point?" I demand.

"My dad could walk in that door every other weekend like he's scheduled to do. Nothing's stopping him. But he's as gone as your mother." She blinks at me several times, and I try to catch up. She's not talking about my mom. Not really. She's talking about her dad. Obviously, the conversation with Charlotte downstairs hit Briella harder than I'd expected. To hear her talk about her dad is strange. I'd always just thought of him as the goose that always came up with that golden egg just when it was needed. An invisible goose.

I don't answer her, don't know how to. Briella's never talked to me about her dad before, and it's obvious from the look on her face now, she's regretting it. She backs up toward the open door.

"I'm just saying you're not the only one with issues, Ever." She shakes her head like she's trying to clear the craziness of actually having a conversation with me. "Forget it."

She doesn't really expect you to feel sorry for her. She knows you only think about yourself," Skinny whispers.

Who would feel sorry for someone who looks like Briella?

My stepsister swallows hard, looks away from me. She's said too much, but it's like she can't stop. "My dad makes it clear every single weekend that it was his choice to leave," she says, "but that doesn't mean I'm going to lie around in my bed and eat myself to death."

"You think I want this?" My hands contract into fists by my sides. Suddenly, it isn't about my mom or her dad. It's all about me.

"Yeah, I think you do. You'd do something about it if you didn't. It's not like you're in a wheelchair or something like that. You don't have to be fat."

It's what every thin person in the world thinks. I should know. Skinny has whispered it into my ear over and over again.

"People lose weight all the time." Briella flings a ponytail over one shoulder and glares at me. "You eat less and you exercise more. It's science."

"Don't you think I've tried? Diets and exercise don't work for me."

"Then do that surgery. I saw that actress had it. She lost hundreds of pounds. You could do that."

"And it will just magically go away, right?" Everyone thinks there's a simple solution I just haven't thought about yet. Drink protein drinks for breakfast. Eat only apples one day a week. Buy some jiggling dumbbell from an infomercial.

"Yeah." She leans in toward me, excited now with this brilliant idea. "They make your stomach smaller and then you lose a lot of weight."

"Or you die," I say.

She looks confused.

"Sometimes people die when they have that surgery. Of a blood clot or some other complication."

"So you know about it?"

"Do you think I don't watch TV?" She is so amazingly stupid. "How would you like it if someone told you to cut yourself open and rearrange your body parts? That then you could be normal?"

"It'd be better than . . ." her voice trails off, and she realizes she's gone too far.

"Get out, Briella."

"Look, I'm sorry. I didn't mean it."

"Yes, you did," I say. I want to hurt her back, and I know how to do it. "No wonder Lindsey is the popular one. You're The Great Lindsey's little sister, but who are you next year when she leaves for college? You're nobody."

I feel bad the minute it comes out of my mouth. She lowers her eyes, but not before I see the pain. It has hit home. Hard.

"Congratulations. You're fat and mean," Skinny says.

"Never mind. Lie here and do nothing. I don't care." Briella leaves finally, stalking out the door and slamming it behind her.

The noise wakes Roxanne, and she comes back up on the bed. She flops down along the length of my body, lays her head on my stomach, and looks up at me with sad, sympathetic eyes. I rub her silky smooth ears until her eyes close to slits, and she starts to puppy snore.

It doesn't matter what Briella thinks about me. What I am is too far in for her to see. I can't be found. By anyone.

I pull out a half-pound bag of M&M's from under my nightstand drawer, trying not to wake the sleeping dog, and tear it open with my teeth. It's no use. Roxanne's head perks up with the tiniest rustle of the bag, and she turns toward me with a hopeful gaze.

"Chocolate Labs cannot have chocolate," I say for about the hundredth time, and Roxanne flops her head back down on the bed.

I grab a handful of M&M's and pour them into my mouth. My hands are like oven mitts. The fingers indistinguishable from one another. I eat two more handfuls before I slow down. I shove the music back deep into my ears, but it doesn't stop the noise in my head.

It's not like I haven't thought about the surgery before. But if I have the surgery, I could die, and that scares me. I have a door inside my head. It's a black door with big red letters that spell out one word: DEATH. And even though I've kept myself from getting too close, I know something of what's waiting behind that door. It's a black, swirling tornado, like the kind I've seen on TV and in the movies with the cows and the houses swirling around inside all that black wind. But it's different, too, because instead of pulling me up into the sky, it pulls me down, down, down into a world that is different from everything I know — into a world where "is" becomes "was."

Memories of childhood go swirling by mixed with all the

houses and cows and fence posts. And every memory has my mom in it. My mom when I was little, helping me bake cookies for the first time — I got to lick the spoon. My mom bringing out my birthday cake when I was seven — the candles lighting up her beaming face. My mom putting a big yellow trash can underneath my mouth, while holding my hair back from my face, when I was throwing up from too much candy corn at Halloween when I was ten. And at the bottom of that swirling horrible black tornado there is no mom.

Even worse than the dying part, is the hoping. If I hope for normal, and it doesn't happen, then what? I lose five pounds. Ten pounds. Hope raises its ugly head, and I start to believe. I can do it. I can lose the weight. I can be normal. But then something happens. It starts to go back the other way. One pound. I slip up. Five pounds. I try to make it stop. I can't. Ten pounds. Don't. Twenty pounds. I'm back there again. STOP. Thirty pounds. I'm worse off than when I started. I'm hopeless.

It isn't like I can hide it. I wear my failure for everyone to see. When the diet fails and the pounds come back, I know what they think.

I knew she couldn't do it.

I told you.

So sorry.

Too bad.

Look at her.

Pity from the kindest. Gloating from the rest.

Tears roll out the corners of my eyes and down my face to the pillow, leaving wet, salty patches of pity for myself. I pull up the blankets over the mass of my body. I'm so tired of looking at my prison.

I turn out the light and try to escape into my dreams. *Wicked* plays me out.

PRINCE CHARMING

CHAPTER FOUR

I'm in line for the spring awards ceremony right between Wolfgang Gines and Kristen Rogers. Kristen is in front of me. I focus on the back of her head, her naturally curly, soft brown hair cascading down to the middle of her back. Kristen's mom, retired stripper Crystal Rogers, offers free pole-dancing classes on Sunday afternoons if you bring your church bulletin. Of course, you have to wear clothes, and she dances only to "Christian music."

I glance back at Wolfgang. He shifts from one foot to the other, staring over the top of my head. Like he doesn't see me. Right.

"He can't believe he has to sit by you. He's going to be telling his football buddies about this at practice today," Skinny says.

I can't really blame him. It's pretty obvious I'm not going to fit. They put the wooden folding chairs lined up right next to one another. Touching. There won't be room. Kristen is normal high-school-girl sized. Probably doesn't weigh more than a hundred twenty-five pounds. I can use some of her space. Wolfgang won't be as easy, though. He's big — the football-player, camouflage-hat-wearing, take-off-from-school-the-first-day-of-hunting-season type. His family currently supports a bill to allow legally blind hunters to use laser sights to hunt any game sighted people can hunt. He was quoted in the Huntsville *Item* as saying, "This opens up the fun of hunting to additional people, and I think that's great." C'mon, what's not to like? A bunch of blind people out in the forest shooting guns?

Wolfgang's going to need all of his seat space and more.

Kristen glances back at me, flipping a few curls over her shoulder with a signature move, and frowns. Her light brown eyes are the same exact color as her hair.

"You've got to be kidding me. Out of all the kids in this line, I have to be next to her?"

I stick my tongue out at her and she quickly turns back to face front with a huffy puffy noise.

There is a rustle of people and voices out beyond the curtains. The whole school will be here. It's required. The bleachers will be full of students all the way up to the nosebleed section. The band will play, the principal will speak, some class president will say a few words, and they will announce the awards.

"Are your hands shaking?" It takes me a minute to realize Wolfgang is talking over my head to Kristen. "What's wrong with you?"

"I don't like to be in front of crowds," she mumbles back to him. "Stage fright."

She should take one of her mom's classes. Hanging upside down on a pole would probably give her plenty of confidence.

I see Rat near the back of the line with the other science geeks. He gives me a silent thumbs-up, and I nod back at him. Since I'm only receiving the award for outstanding sophomore English student, I don't actually have to go to the podium. That's the only reason I actually came to this thing. Otherwise, I would have faked being sick or something to get out of it. But they told me all I had to do was sit there and smile when my name was announced. They said I didn't even have to stand up. But I didn't think about the wooden chairs in tight little lines waiting out there in the stage lights. It was a stupid mistake.

Once when I was nine years old I sang a solo. It was Christmas Eve, and the church was lit only with candles. I sang "O Holy Night." There was a collectively murmured "awww" when I walked slowly to the center of the stage. They thought I was cute and chubby, and they were going to like it no matter what sound came out of my mouth because I was a kid and it was Christmas.

Then I sang the first line. I could feel the surprise trickle through the crowd. I could actually sing. Pure. Clear. Perfect. On the first chorus, I hit the high note. *O night divine!* I felt like an electrical plug meeting a socket for the first time. The energy surged through me, connecting me directly to every single person in every single pew. I had them, all of them, held in the notes soaring through the wooden beams of the chapel. People wanted to look at me because they wanted to listen to me. My body dissolved into the sound.

Magical and totally addictive. I knew that night it was what I was meant to do. Sing. There was no one in the room who doubted it.

Especially not me.

Then the music was trapped inside the pounds, and I stopped singing. Now I can only remember what it felt like to want people to watch me.

I see Jackson in the front row of the trombones. He has on his football jersey. Number 82. Not many boys play football and are in the band. That's part of his charm. He's a geeky jock. Perfect.

I watch him laughing and talking with two flute players in front of him. He is so relaxed. So easy. His smile flashes often, and the flute players respond with giggles. One girl, the one with the little red rectangle glasses, hugs him, still laughing. I wonder what it feels like to reach out unselfconsciously and touch — randomly, casually, and frequently.

"You'll never know," Skinny says softly. *"Never, Ever."*

Kristen steps in front of me and sits down in an empty seat. I squeeze down into the space beside her, breathing in and out shallowly. It hurts to watch, but I can't stop. I focus on Jackson's face and try to feel smaller in the wooden folding chair. I cross my arms tightly over my chest and press my thighs together. The less room I take up the better. Hundreds and hundreds of eyes stare down at me from rows and rows of bleachers. Take a breath. Another. Concentrate on being invisible. And smaller.

"God, she takes up so much space. Just look at those thighs. I can't believe her fat is touching me."

Kristen scoots to the far side of her chair away from me, nervously twisting a strand of hair around and around her finger. I cross my arms even tighter over my chest and pinch my arm between my thumb and finger. Harder. The pain helps me focus on something besides the eyes.

The gym is as quiet as it's going to get. The principal, a middle-aged man with a forehead that stretches well over the top of his head, walks to the podium and taps the microphone a couple times. After a few attempts at getting the top rows of students to stop talking, he introduces the junior class president. She is a black-haired girl wearing silver hooped earrings that swing back and forth as she marches up to the mic. Her name is Tracey Bolton, and she's never said a word to me. Skinny's filled me in on what she thinks about me, which isn't much.

Tracey places a couple of typed pages on the podium, and I see her hands shaking. She's practiced long and hard for this moment in the spotlight. When she starts to speak, I have to admit I'm surprised. Her voice, unlike her hands, doesn't quiver.

"Principal Brown, members of the School Board, teachers, parents, friends, and fellow classmates, it is an honor to speak to all of you today. Go Hornets!"

I slowly stretch my feet out in front of me, trying to make myself longer. Leaner. It isn't working. Kristen makes a big huffy noise.

"God. You are a cow!" Skinny fills in her thoughts.

I tune out a couple of sentences into Tracey's speech. I watch Jackson.

Back when we were ten we'd never seen snow before. So when the weatherman announced the possibility, it was like Christmas came early. There was a buzz everywhere. Grocery stores, sidewalks, libraries, and, most of all, school. Everyone wanted to talk about the weather and the possibility of snow.

When it actually happened, I was stunned. I opened my upstairs bedroom curtain to see everything coated in white. I hardly slept the night before, wishing for the possibility. My mom came in and told me the even better news: School had been canceled. I did a snow dance in my bedroom. It was perfect. I thought it couldn't be a more perfect day. I was wrong.

Jackson knocked on the door around ten that morning. I dug up every piece of winter clothes I could find and met him at the door with rubber rain boots and two gloves that didn't match. I had on two sweaters, a coat a size too small, and three pairs of socks. I walked like a mummy rising from the dead. Jackson had a hooded sweatshirt on over several layers that made him look like a pillow-top mattress. His eyes were bright with excitement, and he clapped his red-gloved hands together and stomped off his boots on my porch.

The sun sparkled off the white piles of snow on the bare branches of the trees, making starlike shimmers of ice. The few orange leaves left on the tree limbs drooped off the brown sticks in surrender. Every once in a while a big plop of snow fell out of the tops, reminding us both that the melting had already started. We had to enjoy it fast.

"This is your opportunity to make a difference in the world . . . blah blah blah," Tracey drones from the podium.

The air was visible everywhere. Puffs from our mouths, from cars, from the tops of houses. Little white clouds of excitement. The cold made our cheeks pink, and I had to blink the dryness out of my eyes. A flake landed, like a frozen moment in time, on Jackson's thick, black lashes. He blinked, but it stayed stubbornly in place. I reached up to brush it off. My throat ached from breathing in the air, but I didn't mind.

I remember crunching down the sidewalk toward the soccer field, delighted with the double trail of boot prints left behind. No one had been there before us. Not even a rabbit or a squirrel. It was a white stretch of untouched fun. We stomped out into the field, laughing and slip-sliding on an icy undercoat of grass. Jackson scooped up a big pile of powder and plopped it down on my head. I squealed and rolled away, reaching for my revenge scoop to push down the back of his sweatshirt.

The fight was on. I ducked behind a park bench and just missed a flying snowball that broke up into a fine mist of powder as it hit a tree trunk behind my head. I waggled my fingers beside my face and stuck my tongue out at him.

"You're going to get it now!" he yelled.

"You couldn't hit the side of a barn," I yelled back.

I ran, and he chased me. Catching me by the soccer goals, he grabbed me around the waist, and we rolled onto the field. Lying on our backs, the cold seeping beneath our layers of clothes, we gasped for breath. I opened my mouth at the sky and stretched out my tongue. A perfectly aimed snowflake drifted down and landed on its outstretched tip. I glanced over at Jackson. He was watching me so intently, so strangely. He rolled over suddenly, heavy with all his layers of clothes on top of me, his hands outstretched to clasp mine in the snow. He looked down at me.

"How did it taste?" he asked.

I could hardly breathe, but it had nothing to do with the cold now. "Wet," I said.

The sun shining over the top of his head left a shimmer behind like a halo. I narrowed my eyes to see him better. His face was so close. His cheeks so red with the cold, his eyelashes wet and spiky. I wanted to push his hair out of his eyes, but he held my hands down into the snow on each side of my body. And I didn't want him to move. I didn't want to do anything to make him move.

"My nose is cold," I said, because I needed to say something.

I thought he would laugh and roll off of me. I thought that would be the end of things. Instead, he leaned in even closer. Closer. And then he kissed the tip of my nose. Very softly.

I blinked up at him in amazement.

He kissed me again. This time on the lips. Soft at first and then a little more urgent. Our cold lips melded together in a frozen moment of absolute perfection.

Now I watch him across the crowded gymnasium pulling at the ponytail of the blond flute player who sits in front of him. The snow day was a long time ago, but I remember. Every detail, every day since. And I wonder, how could he have forgotten?

"As we move forward toward graduation and our lives to come . . . blah blah blah." I'm vaguely aware Tracey is still speaking into the microphone.

No warning. One minute I'm a million miles away in a snow-covered field tasting flakes on my tongue and Jackson's lips on mine. The next minute I am sitting on top of a broken wooden chair in a crowded high school gym. My teeth snap together with the force of the fall, my head jerking upward. A collective gasp echoes through the rafters. Rows and rows of horrified eyes stare down at me.

I'm no longer in the chair. I'm on the floor. I'm on the floor. I try to take it in.

The sound of the crash echoes. The speech stops. The chatter stops. The world stops. All eyes focus on the fat girl sitting on top of the crushed remains of what was once a wooden chair. Kristen stares down at me from her seat with a horrified expression of absolute disbelief. By sitting beside me somehow the ultimate humiliation has spread to her.

"Oh. My. God," she whispers, mortified.

I look beyond her — up and up to the rows of shocked eyes.

Tracey stumbles over her speech but somehow keeps going. I know she will never forgive me for spoiling her moment.

A teacher jumps out from behind the curtain, leaning over me.

"Are you hurt?"

"No," I say, struggling to my feet. "I'm fine."

Tracey keeps going at the microphone. "Our lives will be forever changed by our high-school experiences." You think?

Another teacher pulls a chair out from somewhere. He puts it behind me and I have no choice but to sit down, though I'm careful not to lean back. All I want to do is leave. Run as fast as my fat little legs can carry me. Behind the curtains and out of sight of all the eyes. But I can't leave. So I sit there. My legs shake from the strain of trying to not put any weight on the chair, and I try to ignore Skinny's voice in my ear.

"I knew that would happen one day. Did you see that fat girl? I can't believe I just saw that. Wonder if anybody got that on video — got to post it online!"

My eyes are full of tears, but I will not cry. I've already done enough to draw attention to myself. But there is one thing I can't stop myself from doing. I look at Jackson. He is staring at me now. Just like everyone else in the gym.

"He feels sorry for you. He thinks you're pitiful."

I look away, down at the floor in front of me, feeling like I have a huge red target right over my heart.

I feel Wolfgang shift restlessly in the chair beside me, and he glances over quickly. His look is intense.

"Every hunter knows you have to kill something when it is wounded. It's just a question of how deep the wound goes before it's put out of its misery," Skinny says softly in my ear. *"There's a point when he realizes the poor thing is so wounded it can no longer be fixed."*

I bite my bottom lip until I taste the blood. I'm not at that point. I can be fixed. I clench my hands into fists at my side. There is still something alive deep inside of me. I can feel it beating against my rib cage with iridescent shades of ruby and amethyst wings. The next time I'm on a stage and people are looking at me, it will be different. Jackson will look at me the way he looked at Gigi. I will be in the spotlight — to sing for everyone and to hear only applause.

"Are you crazy? There aren't parts like that for fat girls like you."

Then I won't be fat.

The idea of talking back to Skinny is appalling. Something I've never done before.

But it's a simple solution, really. Girl loves boy. Boy loves girl. Girl gets fat. Boy leaves. Girl cuts her stomach up into a little bitty pouch to get boy back.

"You will die," Skinny hisses in my ear.

I don't care. If I die, I die. I will do whatever it takes. I will let them cut my stomach open and change my internal organs forever. Even if I have to have a stomach the size of an egg for the rest of my life, I will never feel this way again.

I focus my whole being on trying not to cry. I don't hear the speech at the microphone or the applause that comes from the crowd. I don't hear the principal calling out the names for the awards. I only hear one sound in my ear. I've never heard it before, but it bounces off the inside of my brain and pounds against my ears.

It's Skinny, and she's laughing and laughing and laughing.

CHAPTER FIVE

About two weeks after the chair incident, I have my first appointment for the surgery. Dad goes with me. They do a lot of tests, and we fill in a ton of paperwork, and then sit silently in the waiting room until a tall, silver-haired nurse comes in with a laptop. She's wearing a headband with a sparkly pink bow on top that would have been more appropriate for an eight-year-old, but she's old like a grandmother. She says hello to my dad, but talks to me.

"Have you tried to lose weight before?" she asks.

I nod.

"How?"

I tell her about Weight Watchers when I was nine and fat camp when I was eleven. I tell her about cutting carbs and counting calories. She types it all down on her computer. Silently. I don't tell her about the cabbage diet or the lemon water diet or the cayenne pepper diet, because that's just crazy.

My dad throws in the hypnotherapist I went to see down in Conroe when I was twelve. I forgot about that one.

I could have added more, but she closes her laptop and stands up. "The doctor will be in to see you shortly," she says over her shoulder as she leaves.

A few minutes later, a man knocks on the door and comes in with his hand extended to my dad. Thin, dark-haired, with a beard, he could have played Abe Lincoln in a school play with only the addition of a tall black hat. He sits down on a rolling stool, and my dad and I listen to exactly what will happen to my insides. My brain feels cluttered and cramped. My dad frowns the whole time and asks a lot of questions.

"Why can't she take nutrition classes or something like that instead?"

The doctor looks over at me. "How many calories is a Big Mac?" he asks.

"Five hundred and sixty," I answer automatically.

He nods. "How many calories do you need to eat every day to maintain a weight of three-hundred-and-two pounds?"

"Three thousand, two hundred and eighty."

The doctor turns back to my dad. "She doesn't need a class," he says.

"Isn't she too young for this, Dr. Wilkerson?"

"With obesity on the rise among sixteen- to nineteen-year-olds, many doctors have begun approving the surgery for teens — the youngest on record being twelve years old." The doctor smiles at me, but his eyes look too busy to really focus.

"How did you let yourself get in this condition? Obese teenagers. It's a national epidemic."

"Because she is only fifteen, you will need to sign that you give your permission." The doctor holds out a clipboard and pen to my dad. Dad hesitates.

"What if she doesn't do it?" he asks, his empty hand hovering above the paper. "What if I say no?"

The doctor looks from me back to my dad. "This isn't about looking good in your jeans. Morbidly obese teenagers turn into overweight adults with a reduced life expectancy." He glances down at the folder in his hand. "Your daughter already has signs of high blood pressure. She could also develop diabetes and heart problems."

I swallow hard. He's talking about me. Reduced life expectancy. Morbid obesity. My head is floating, disconnected from my body.

"It's okay, Dad," I say. My voice cracks a little, but I cover it up with a small cough. "This is what I want."

My father nods and reaches for the pen, but his hand shakes a little when he signs his name in an erratic scrawl on the bottom line.

"It's good you're here," the doctor says to my dad. "Obesity surgery is a major undertaking, and it's really important that your family be well educated about the procedure, the expected consequences, and potential problems."

"Her stepmother would be here with us, too, but she had to work. We're all in this together — the whole family,"

Dad says. I wonder if he's checked with Briella and Lindsey about that.

"Good." The doctor looks at me directly now, brown eyes unblinking behind his wire-rimmed glasses. "Because weight-loss surgery and the way it changes your life will affect your entire household. You will need everyone's support to be as successful as possible."

From his folder he pulls out a colored flyer, props it on one knee, and reads it out loud. "In gastric bypass procedures, a smaller stomach pouch is formed in the upper portion of the stomach and a new stomach outlet is formed. After the intestine is divided, the lower intestine is connected to the new stomach outlet."

All the words surround and smother me. I can't breathe. I bite my lower lip to feel the pain and nod like I completely understand what he's talking about. But I don't. Not really.

"This definitely isn't something to be taken lightly," the doctor adds. "Surgical risks from operating on the stomach and intestines can include infection, suture leaks, and blood clots. Changes to the digestive tract may cause ulcers, bowel obstruction, or reflux."

"Great," I say, sarcastically. Realizing it doesn't come out very enthusiastically, I clear my throat and try again. "I'm very excited. What's next?" I ask, trying to sound ready to go even though my stomach feels like a shaken-up Coke.

"Before you can schedule your surgery, you must attend a dietary education session and a pre-op educational support group. We also strongly encourage you to bring a buddy or family member with you." I wonder who I'll take. "The seminar will be facilitated by the surgeon and staff members. You'll have all the time you need to ask all of your questions about your post-operative diet and follow-up care."

On the way out of the office, I'm handed a big blue folder with the words GASTRIC SPECIALISTS OF CENTRAL TEXAS stamped on the front in gold letters. I open it up and flip through the pages of materials included. Pre-surgery, post-surgery, diet, food lists. My stomach lurches again. I'm overwhelmed. I close the folder again and mumble my thanks to the receptionist.

That night, with my bedroom door shut tightly, I slide my laptop out from under my bed and log in quickly. I go to the bookmarked site as soon as the wireless connects. It's labeled "Shoes" on my favorites bar even though the likelihood of someone caring enough to search my computer is next to nothing. It should be labeled "Fatties" because it's a home for the masses out there looking for weight-loss surgery to save them from their blubber prisons. I click on the forum, "Teen Patients." I've been coming here for almost a year now.

Trying to hang in there. Just can't figure out what is wrong with me and why this is working so much better for others on here and not working so good for me. THANKS for the encouragement.

Don't give up!! Next month will be two years for me. I know it is hard not to, but celebrate what you have achieved and what is yet to come. You can do it! If I can, you can. I started at 249, this morning was 107. This surgery was the best thing I could have done for myself. Hang in there.

Was 284 Pounds!!! Holy Beep!!! Size 22/24 2X/3X WHO WAS THAT GIRL??? Now — 169 pounds!! 5'7" size 4/6 tops and 9/10 bottoms. I did NOT lose any muscle mass and my body fat is 33%!! Now I know what it feels like to cross my legs and to fit in an airplane seat.

I was told yesterday that my throat is totally inflamed and food is now going into my lungs. I have pneumonia due to the inflammation. They also said this IS life threatening. Help! Anyone else had this happen??

I scroll through the postings, reading until my head is buzzing with the words of the escapees. Some have made it out into the sunshine. Some are still trapped in the tunnel they dug for themselves. I don't know which one I'll be, but I know I can't stay locked away in my prison of fat for the rest of my life. I shut off the computer and slide it back under the bed. I put the packet from the doctor's office under there, too, and turn out the light. Looking up at the ceiling, I can still feel the chorus of voices seeping out from the website. Sad. Joyous. Defeated. Angry. Amazed. Hopeful. My headphones lie on the nightstand, but I know there is no music that can drown them out.

I don't go to sleep for a very long time.

It's a good thing I didn't chuck the folder in the trash, even though I wanted to. It comes in handy a couple of weeks later when Rat and I go to the session.

Dad is on a business trip, and Charlotte is helping sponsor the cheerleader fund-raising car wash. Lindsey is busy with senior parties and graduation plans, and who knows where Briella is. So Rat volunteers to be my support buddy and everyone happily agrees.

Rat's the only one, other than my family, who knows what's happening. At first I feel bad that Rat has to go with me — like it's got to be a burden. But he launches himself into all the material in the big blue folder like it's some kind of bestselling novel. He's completely fascinated with every single page of the reading material, especially all the gory medical details. To him the whole experience is an exotic science experiment, complete with various charts and graphs for future data entry of my weight loss.

Unfortunately for me, Rat has a perfect recall of anything he reads, so he happily recites various quotes from the Blue

Folder on the drive to the meeting. I don't need him to make me more nervous, but with typical Rat obliviousness, he doesn't notice.

"They will make two small incisions. Then they insert the camera with the light on the end into one of the holes in your stomach. Did you know that it's really dark inside the human body?" He is talking and driving way too fast. Way too excited.

"Never really thought about it before," I say. Rat is especially interested in the actual surgery, which is the part that makes me feel nauseated.

"They pump your abdomen full of gas so they can move around in there and then they put the instrument through the other hole. That's how they get to your stomach."

"So they are going to give me gas?" I try to distract him with a little joke, but it doesn't work.

"Only you won't call it a stomach anymore," he says. "It's a pouch."

"Now I'm a kangaroo?" I mumble. It doesn't slow him down. He whips into the parking lot and turns down the row looking for a space.

"The pouch is designed to hold approximately one table-spoon of solid, unchewed food. Your teeth compress the food to about one-fourth of its unchewed volume."

"Fascinating," I say. I point out an empty parking spot. "There's one."

"So, if you chew everything up really well, you can hold approximately three tablespoons of food in your new pouch, which would be about the size of a golf ball or a hard-boiled egg."

Three tablespoons of food? That's all? It should be scary enough to make me turn back, but it isn't. Nor is the first thing I glimpse when I enter the conference room: a scale.

A tiny woman with a fuzzy white halo of hair measures my height and checks my vital signs. Rat follows along with a little green notepad and records everything. I squint my eyes to let him know how serious I am, then try to mouth the words for him to go sit down, but he ignores me. The scale gets closer, and Rat stays glued to my side. I start to feel panicky, my breath coming in short little puffs. Don't make me do this. Don't make me do this. Don't. Make. Me. Do. This.

"Go away," I say, but Rat is already waiting beside the scale with his notepad in hand.

"I have to record the starting point," Rat says, flipping the paper over to a new page.

"Please," I whisper, not ready for this part. Not wanting Rat to see what's coming. "I can tell you what I weigh. You don't have to measure it now."

"Get up on the scale," the fuzzy-haired woman says, smiling kindly but totally ignoring my pleas to Rat. She's probably heard every excuse in the book, and she's not buying it. I take a deep breath and step onto the hated metal platform. She slides the weights over and over and then over again until they finally balance at 302 pounds. Rat peers over her shoulder, and I wait for the gasp of horror.

"Oh my God. I can't believe a human being can weigh this much!" Skinny whispers Rat's thoughts in my ear and I cringe with embarrassment.

I glance over at Rat, my cheeks hot with shame, but he is evidently able to keep his disgust well hidden. He never looks up as he records the weight in his notebook.

After I complete a survey about my eating habits and finish the check-in process, I look around, and Rat is nowhere to be found. Now that I actually want him with me, he disappears? I mumble, "Jerk," under my breath and try to find two empty chairs in the rows of seats. I sit on the end so I don't have to be squashed up against other people and put my purse in the seat next to me. Rat will probably show up again soon. In the meantime, I glance around the room. There are about ten other people. It's easy to tell who is there for the surgery and who is there for the support. I'm definitely the youngest in the room.

A huge woman wearing purple stretch pants slides slowly into a seat in the row in front of me. Plastic tubes are attached to her nose and lead down to an oxygen tank on wheels at her side. She isn't that old, but she breathes so heavily I can hear her rhythmic gasps for breath. The acne-faced teenage boy with her leans over to ask if she's all right. She nods, but she can't say anything. The effort of walking into the room has made her so short of breath, she can't speak.

"That will be you. Soon . . . soon."

I don't want to keep looking at purple-pants woman. It just

makes me sad. I twist around in my chair, looking desperately for Rat and finally see him over in the corner talking to my doctor. He's scribbling frantically in his notebook, nodding, while Dr. Wilkerson talks. I try to catch his eye, but he is as oblivious as ever.

The fuzzy-haired woman steps up to the podium and welcomes the crowd. The others applaud, and Rat looks up from his notebook at last. I motion frantically for him to come sit down. He writes in his notebook all the way over to the seat, but at least he finally joins me.

Fuzzy-haired woman introduces Dr. Wilkerson, or Abe Lincoln as I think of him, and then takes her place behind a waiting projector. The doctor steps up to the stage, welcomes everybody, and the small crowd again applauds politely. The first slide shows up on the pull-down screen, and Dr. Wilkerson gets immediately into the nitty-gritty of why we're all here, pointing toward the drawing of a stomach on the slide.

Rat continues scribbling in his notebook. Sometimes drawing pictures, sometimes making various grunting noises in agreement. I try to ignore him.

The doctor goes on about small intestines and absorption. This is the second time I've heard this explanation, but I still can't really take it all in. I narrow my eyes and try to focus on the steady onslaught of medical terminology. Biology was never my favorite class. I can't tell the difference between a stomach and a kidney, but I do understand that my insides will never look the same again.

Forever.

Rat's hand shoots up. I roll my eyes and slouch down in my chair. Really?

"So exactly what are the advantages of gastric bypass surgery?" he asks when the doctor points to him.

"Well, as you can see" — Dr. Wilkerson points to the picture behind him and Rat nods — "the procedure reduces the amount of food absorbed by the body, resulting in rapid weight loss in the first six months following the surgery."

Several people in the audience nod. Rapid weight loss. That's what we all want to hear, and it's worth all the rest that is to come. But hope is such a fragile flower in the rocky ground of my soul. I don't know how to nurture it and I'm shocked at its appearance.

"You will be the one person that doesn't lose weight. You'll do everything like they say, but you'll still be the same. You can't change," she whispers. I should have known Skinny wouldn't miss this.

"Of course, this limits the amount of food that can be eaten at any one time and it controls the intake of high-calorie sweets and fats due to dumping syndrome," Dr. Abe Lincoln goes on.

Huh? What was that? No sweets?

The doctor continues, "Eating high-fat or high-sugar foods can cause nausea and weakness when sweets enter the bloodstream too quickly due to intestinal changes."

"Hummmm . . ." Rat says. He writes "no sweets" on his paper and underlines it three times.

No more M&M's? No more ice cream? Hey, wait a minute.

"So what are the disadvantages?" Rat asks. I'm still grieving the loss of M&M's and am thinking that's a pretty big disadvantage. Of course, Rat has glossed right over that little detail and is now on to the grim medical facts.

Rat writes each one of the risks on his paper with a star in the margin to bullet each point. Each one basically means I could die or be in pain for the rest of my life. And I have the most life left to live out of everyone in this room. I'm choosing to do this to myself? I glance around and wonder for a moment if all of us will be happy with our decision. Will someone in this room not survive the surgery? I can almost hear a roulette wheel spinning around above our heads, waiting to drop the death marble into a slot. Will it click into the slot for purple-pants woman? The Weeble-shaped man in the stretched-to-the-limit blue jeans in the front row? Or maybe . . . me?

"You'll also be left with a lifetime need for nutritional supplements to avoid vitamin and mineral deficiencies, which can lead to serious health conditions, including metabolic bone disease or anemia."

Yeah, yeah. So I take Flintstones vitamins. No big deal. It's the dying and pain part that I keep thinking about . . . and the loss of M&M's. The woman in front of me's breathing machine sucks the air in and out with a rhythmic, never-ending push-pull. Purple-pants woman or death? What are my choices?

At the end of the presentation, the doctor introduces a young man in the front row. He looks about twenty-five with black curly hair and smiling brown eyes. He's wearing blue jeans and a gray T-shirt. A picture of a fat boy comes up on the screen. Only the black curly hair looks the same. The eyes are brown, but they certainly aren't smiling.

"This is me one year ago," he says, gesturing to the screen over his shoulder, "when I weighed almost four hundred pounds."

Now, he looks totally normal.

A year is not that long, I think, looking down at my hands clenched tight in my lap. One year. Three hundred sixty-five days. A tiny spark glows in my head. Things could be different. My life could change. In a year, I could try out for the lead in next year's spring musical. I could be center stage singing for a crowd of people. In the spotlight. No one laughing at me. Jackson would be in the audience looking at me like he looks at Gigi now. The world would be different. A year from now.

The audience of fat people claps like the young man at the podium has just won the Academy Award. He smiles broadly.

"This surgery changed my life. It isn't easy, but it is worth it."

The raw desperation from the people around me leaks out into the room. This is their salvation. A year seems like nothing to those of us trapped inside our bodies. They want to believe it and, I'm so scared to admit it even to myself, I want to believe it, too. If I don't do the surgery, where will I be a year from now? Four hundred pounds? Five hundred? I can't stop it by myself. I know that.

Later that night, I'm in my bed waiting to fall asleep. Maybe it's because I'm close to leaving consciousness or maybe it's because of the curly-haired man at the podium at the meeting earlier, but I let my mind drift. I count up twelve months from now, and I imagine a world for me that's different. I'd have something to look forward to next in my life — a next first day of school, a next Thanksgiving, a next Christmas, a next musical away. There is a strange lifting feeling in my heart. I recognize it and try to push it back down again. It's an idea — a dream — that something could change. Three hundred and sixty-five days from now.

I will be sixteen. I'll go to the Fall Ball with Jackson. I'll wear a strapless red dress and high heels. He'll touch me. I'll dance. At school, I'll walk the halls in miniskirts and black knee-high boots. I'll laugh. I'll sing in front of people. They'll clap and cheer and throw flowers onto the stage. I'll bow.

Next summer, a year from now, will I wear shorts and sleeveless tops? So different from the stretchy jeans I wear now, even in the hottest days of summer, and the black size 5X T-shirts. Will I finally feel the sun on my skin? Will I uncover my legs from all the clothes I've kept my body hidden under? I wonder.

All of it is right in front of me. Only a year away.

"Don't."

Then I stop wondering and start to actually want. I want to go swimming.

"Don't."

I want to learn how to drive a car.

"Don't do it."

I want to climb the stairs and not be out of breath.

"Don't want."

I want to stand in front of that crowd at next year's musical and have them clap at my success.

But then right before I let myself drift off to sleep, I hear it. A whisper in my dreamy, sleepy ear. Louder. Louder. Louder.

"It will never happen."

CHAPTER SIX

The surgery is scheduled for three weeks before school is out. May 2 at 8:00 A.M. to be exact. It would have been better if I'd been able to finish the semester, but evidently surgeons don't care too much about summer break. I have to cut my stomach up on their schedule.

Because of my grades, I'm able to get myself out of pretty much everything. My average is high enough to be exempt from final projects, and I arrange to do all the other work ahead of time. All my teachers seem fine with my upcoming absence. Especially when I'm sufficiently vague about my medical issues. They really don't want to ask a lot of questions. Mr. Blair is the only teacher left to talk to, so I hang around after the bell on Friday.

I lean against the wall, waiting for him to explain the home-work assignment to Kristen Rogers for the third time.

"Are you next?" It's Jackson. He gestures toward Kristen and Mr. Blair.

"Go ahead," I say. "I'm not in a rush."

"Great. Thanks." He smiles at me as he slides into place between me and the teacher's desk. "I just have a quick question about number three on the homework and I can't be late to spring training. The coach will kill me."

"I see some things haven't changed." I smile back at him. Next week everything's going to change, but I don't say anything about that. I just want him to remember how things were.

His head tilts to the side and he looks at me quizzically. "What do you mean?"

"You were always the last one to show up to everything," I say. "You know . . . when we were kids."

Remember. I plead with him silently.

His dark brows draw together over those beautiful blue eyes as if he's thinking hard about it. "I guess so," he finally says.

"He has no idea what you're talking about," Skinny says.

He turns back toward Mr. Blair's desk, tapping his pencil against the notebook in his hands to fill the sudden silence. I'm left staring at his broad shoulders in front of me, thinking of the past.

Sometimes on those spring nights when we were kids, Rat, Jackson, and I would chase one another with flashlights in the open space behind our back fences. We played until the hamburgers were finished grilling on the outside patio and our moms called us to dinner or until the moon rose so high in the sky that hiding in the dark was almost impossible.

The game went like this. If you were "it," you won the game by shining the flashlight onto the hidden person like a spotlight. They'd have to freeze in the position you spotted them — arms stretched out, legs crouched, mouth wide open — until you released them with a click of the flashlight. If you weren't "it," there was only one place you could be safe from the flashlight's beacon and only one way you could win the game. If you could successfully hide from the spotlight long enough to make it to the big boulder out near the walking trail, climb atop it, and proclaim loud enough for everyone in hearing distance, all the open back windows and sliding patio doors that surrounded our little piece of wild, "Home free!" — then you were the winner.

I picture Jackson, atop that granite boulder, arms outstretched above his head. In my mind I see him punching his clenched fists at the carpet of twinkling stars overhead with a look of absolute delight on his face shouting, "Home free!"

Don't you remember? I think.

I fidget with the cover on my notebook, trying to collect my thoughts, and desperately search for words of the past that will trigger the memories. I think about how we used to lie for hours in the grass out by the soccer fields and look at clouds. Rat saw cirrus and stratus clouds. I saw circles and triangles. Jackson saw bunnies and alligators and pipe-smoking old men. He was the best at finding something out of the white clumps of nothingness. When he was older, he was going to become a pilot and fly right through those clouds, he'd tell us.

"Do you still like planes?" I blurt out into the sudden silence.

Look at me, Jackson, I want to say. Look for the something inside *this* clump of nothingness.

He turns back around to glance down at me. Finally. But he still has the same puzzled expression on his face.

"Sure," he says, vaguely.

"You had all those models of planes in your basement." I don't give up. I need to see the recognition in his eyes now. Before the surgery next week changes me forever. "You wanted to be a pilot."

He laughs. "I don't have much time for airplane models these days. With football and band and" He motions toward Mr. Blair's desk. ". . . homework."

"You wouldn't understand," Skinny hisses in my ear. *"You just hang around the house eating yourself into a stupor."*

"I guess you're really busy," I say.

"And I have to get a workout in there somewhere or I'm never going to make varsity." He flexes his arm. His bicep bulges against the short sleeve of his T-shirt. The height and the muscles are new this year. He doesn't look the same, but I haven't forgotten what he's like on the inside. And his eyes are exactly the same. I know those blue-green eyes with the darkly fringed lashes. I've seen them crinkled with laughter, muddled with fever, sparking with anger, and squinting in pain. I saw those eyes when they were blue-green with delight at his first time on a skateboard. And when they were gray-green and clouded with tears over the death of his cat, Mr. Whiskers.

Once they were even black-green when they glittered at me from behind a Spider-Man mask on Mr. Peter's front porch. But most of all I remember the deep, grass green of his eyes, intense and compelling, right before I closed mine and kissed him.

Look in my eyes, Jackson. Remember. Me.

But there is no sign of recognition.

Mr. Blair finishes with Kristen and waves Jackson up. I watch as he leans over the desk, listening intently, his rumpled brown hair falling down into his eyes. My hands itch to push it back away from his face, but I just stand there.

Remembering.

ABRACADABRA

CHAPTER SEVEN

What if I don't wake up?" I mumble under my breath.

The annoyingly cheerful woman with the smiley-face scrubs wraps a big rubber band around my arm, ignoring my question completely. She snaps it into a tie above my elbow and slaps my forearm. The fat of my arm jiggles as she frowns down at what she sees.

"That may be a good one there." She prods at my arm, searching for a place to stick the waiting needle.

I try to look sympathetic. I don't know if I should apologize or what. What am I supposed to say? I'm sorry my veins are all covered up in fat just like the rest of me?

"I'll be right back." She's going for help. The first one always goes for help. Everything that is alive and pumping inside of me is somewhere underneath all of this.

"The odds of death are one in two hundred. That's pretty slim," Rat says. He's sitting on the end of the hospital bed in the pre-op room.

"Thanks," I say.

"But I guess if one hundred and ninety-nine people had the surgery this week then . . ." He doesn't smile. He isn't kidding.

"That's not helping."

"Where's your dad?" Rat asks, and I know he's trying to change the subject.

"On his way. Got called in for a traffic accident."

"Bad?" Rat asks. We both know that a town with I-45 running through the middle of it at seventy-five miles an hour always has the potential for deadly accidents.

"Could have been, but it turned out okay. Larry Joe Green's three cases of beer were strapped into the child safety seats instead of his two kids."

Smiley Face returns with a helper and they set to work on my arm again. I feel the prick one more time and then a sharp pain as the needle digs in deeper.

"Ah, there we are. I was afraid for a moment we were going to have to call this whole thing off." Smiley Face laughs like she has just told a hilarious joke. Helper Nurse bustles around the bed, hooking up tubes and bags to my arm. She slides a metal cap over my finger and moves the monitor stand over closer to the bed. Numbers flash on the screen accompanied by an occasional beep. I watch the monitor and hope the line doesn't go flat. I've probably watched too many medical dramas. I know flat lines are not a good thing.

The song playing over and over in my mind is "The Point of No Return" from *The Phantom of the Opera*.

The nurse asks Rat to move over to the chair by the windows. She pushes the thin blanket off my legs and starts fiddling around with my feet. First she pulls a pair of stockings on me, then straps on some leggings over the top.

"These are the hottest things out there." Patting my legs, she smiles at me. "Lovely, aren't they?"

She plugs the leggings into a machine under the bed and they start to fill up with air, squeezing tightly against my calves over and over again with a weird pumping sound. The sound masks the scared panting noise of my breathing.

"It'll help your circulation," Rat says. "So you don't get blood clots."

The nurse looks at him in surprise. "You're a smart boy. Want to be a doctor someday?"

"Not a medical doctor, if that's what you mean," says Rat, "although I will probably get my PhD in nuclear physics."

The nurse doesn't know what to say about that, so she just nods and leaves again. Rat continues to read the booklet we received at the informational session.

"Is this going to work?" My voice shakes a little.

"Probably," says Rat, pushing the glasses back up his nose, his big blue eyes unblinking behind them. "Most people lose from thirteen to twenty pounds in the first month, and most of this weight is lost in the first two weeks because of the diet. It takes about a year to lose the rest."

"But is it going to work for me?"

"The odds are that it will," Rat says solemnly. "It says there is plenty of time for weight loss after the gastric bypass surgery has healed."

And then he smiles. One of those rare "Rat Smiles" that so few people have ever seen. The angles of his face soften, his eyes crinkle, and two huge dimples appear out of nowhere. I could swear you almost hear music like when angels appear in the movies when Rat smiles. It makes me feel better. How could it not?

The curtain pulls back with a squeak, and my dad is there.

"Hey, Mr. Davies."

"Rat." Even my dad doesn't know his real first name. "How's it going here?"

"Good. She's almost ready," Rat reports like he's the doctor in charge. "They have her IV started, and we're waiting for the anesthesiologist." He stands. "Here, take this chair. I need to go to the bathroom."

If it was anyone else, I would think he was being sensitive to leave me and my dad alone for a while. But it's Rat, so I think it probably means he has to go to the bathroom.

He pulls the curtains back and disappears. Dad drags the chair over closer to the bed and sits down.

My dad sent me a letter once when I was thirteen. He actually mailed it to our house. I guess he didn't know how else to get my attention. It was after he tried to say something to me when I took a second piece of chocolate cake after dinner. He looked at me like he'd been looking at me a lot, with this critical, disapproving look.

"He's sorry he has such a fat, ugly daughter." It was the first

time I heard Skinny clearly. She'd been mumbling around inside my mind for a while, but this time her words came out in fully formed sentences. *"You are such an embarrassment."*

"Do you really need that second piece?" my dad had asked.

"Yes," I mumbled around the huge bite I'd stuffed into my mouth, "I do."

I ate every bite. My dad kept glancing over at me with that disgusted look on his face, and I kept stuffing in the forkfuls of chocolate. When it was done, I put the fork down on the smeared plate and stomped upstairs to my room. I pushed my headphones in my ears and turned the *Rent* soundtrack up loud enough to drown out everything else.

The letter came a few days later. I didn't recognize the round, loopy handwriting. I don't think I'd ever seen my dad's handwriting like that. On a single page of notebook paper.

Dear Ever,

The reason I want you to lose weight is because I love you, and I want you to be happy. I want you to fall in love some-day and have children of your own. If that's what you want. I know what boys are like. Finding someone who will take the time to look beyond just your looks might be hard. I want you to have a healthy, long life full of many exciting opportunities. Being overweight may keep you from doing everything you want. That's why I want you to lose weight.

I love you,
Dad

I crumpled the letter into my fist and sat there on my bed for a long time. Finally, I unclenched my fingers and smoothed out the paper. I read it again. It just wasn't fair. God made some people naturally skinny and some people naturally fat. I'd never know how my life would have been different if I'd been one of the ones He made skinny. I didn't know how He chose. This one will be blond, with long thin legs and great skin. This one will be short and fat with legs that rub together when she walks. I just knew I wasn't one of the lucky ones.

"Your father is right. No one is going to love you."

Eventually, I folded the letter into a tiny little square and stuffed it into the bottom back corner of my sock drawer. My dad and I never spoke about it.

Over the next six months I gained fifty more pounds.

"Are you sure you want to do this, peanut?" Dad reaches for my hand across the thin white sheet. "You know I love you no matter what, right?"

"I know, Dad."

"I'd walk right out with you if you want to change your mind."

Are those tears in his eyes? This isn't helping me. "I know, Dad."

"I just wish I could talk to her one more time."

"Who?"

"Your mom."

I look over at him, surprised. I know he misses her, but he's never said anything like this before.

"We used to talk about everything. The good. The bad."

Now my eyes fill with tears.

"I just need to talk to her."

I think of my stepmom. "You can talk to Charlotte." I pat his hand awkwardly.

"Charlotte's great. I'm really lucky she came along . . ." His voice trails off. "But it's not the same."

"I know, Dad."

"She'd know exactly what to say to you right now. She was so good at that." He pats my hand carefully so he doesn't mess up the tubes in my arm. "Remember when you were a kid and were afraid of the dark? I thought you'd never sleep all night in that room by yourself."

"Yes." I smile at the memory. "She always asked me what exactly I was afraid of."

"And you said?"

"One time I was afraid all the door hinges would turn into snakes. One time I was afraid of the seven dwarfs marching down the hall with shovels. One time I said I was afraid of fear itself. I think I heard that one on TV. She never laughed. She never said I was crazy. She would just sigh and lead me back to my room and she'd wait there, on the side of my bed, until my eyes were simply too heavy to keep open anymore."

"Then I'd yell for you to go to sleep," Dad says, "and for your mother to come back to bed and turn out the light."

"But do you know what she'd always tell me before she left?" I ask.

He shakes his head.

"'Your dad's not mad at you. He's just tired.'"

"As usual, she was right."

We sit there for a while in quiet. Waiting. I've never been that great at waiting. Like when I was a kid, and sometimes even now, I could never wait for Christmas. When my mom would leave for the grocery store, I would go under the Christmas tree and carefully unwrap the end of each of my presents just far enough to figure out what was inside. Then I'd wrap them back up again before Mom got back. It actually kind of ruined Christmas, but it took away the whole waiting thing.

The hard thing about waiting is the not knowing how it's going to go. That's what makes me really crazy. It could be great — like the doctor saying the test results are back and all the cancer is gone. Or it could be really bad — like the doctor saying something terrible, something you can't even imagine — but you're just supposed to go about your life like that waiting thing is not hanging over your head every single minute of every single day.

The sound of laughter and murmuring voices drift in from the hallway. Rat comes back and stands beside my dad because there is only one chair in the tiny pre-op room.

"Anything happen while I was gone?" he asks.

"Not really," I say. "We're just waiting."

The curtain is flung open, and the nurse with the smiley-face scrubs is back. This time she is with a tall man with blue baggies on his feet that make a swishing sound when he walks. I wonder if the baggies are to keep the blood off his shoes. That kind of freaks me out. Baggie Man introduces himself as Dr. Boyett, the anesthesiologist, and shakes my dad's hand. He has a big syringe with him and he grins down at me like he has brought me a piece of chocolate birthday cake.

"How you feeling?"

"A little nervous," I say.

"Nervous is normal."

"You'll never be normal."

"Time for the good stuff." Dr. Boyett sticks the big syringe into the tube snaking out of my arm and pushes the plunger. "That should take the edge off."

"How long before I start to feel something?" I ask, but before I can even finish the question, my head starts to feel lighter, like it just floated off my body. "Oh, there it is."

My dad laughs nervously. "That didn't take long."

"Say your good-byes," Smiley Face says. "They'll be here for you any minute."

Rat's face is serious, but he gives me a fake smile and a little wave, then steps back out of the way so my dad can move closer.

A shadow moves behind my father's shoulder. With the fuzziness seeping into my body, I can't see clearly, but I know who it is. My constant companion. I should introduce them.

"There's something I've always wanted to say, Dad."

He leans in and pats the top of my plastic-covered head. "What, peanut?"

I should be worried about something, but I'm not. I feel fine. Better than fine.

"Dad," I say. My mouth is dry. I lick my lips and try again louder. "Dad."

"I'm right here."

"There's this fairy thing that sits on my shoulder and whispers in my ear. Bad things."

"He thinks you're crazy-talking."

Another giant, blue-robed figure comes around the curtain. "You ready to go?" he asks.

"I have to tell my dad something."

"Tell him quick. The operating room is waiting." He unlocks the brakes on the hospital bed.

My dad clears his throat. "I love you, Ever," he says, and kisses me on the cheek.

"I can hear her, Dad. In my ear."

He nods and smiles down at me.

"He thinks it's the drugs."

More people come into the room. I try to focus on my dad, but they start to roll the bed out from behind the curtains and down the hall.

"I'll be here when you get back." He waves at me until the big doors swing shut behind my rolling feet, and he's gone.

"I need to tell him," I mumble.

The operating room is freezing. I know it, but I don't really feel it. People move all around me. Some talk to me. Others don't. They count to three and pull me over onto a flat table. Lying on my back, I squint up at the big lights.

Someone behind my head says, "I'm going to put this mask over your face now, okay?"

I guess I say okay because the mask comes down over my nose and mouth.

"Now count backward from one hundred," the voice behind my head continues.

Obediently I start to count. One hundred . . . ninety-nine . . . ninety-eight . . .

"Her name is Skinny," I say. Then everything goes black.

CHAPTER EIGHT

I am aware of noises around me. I'm moving . . . rolling . . . somewhere. I need to throw up. I try to tell someone, but I can't speak.

"It's okay. You're all right," a woman's voice says in my ear.

I open my eyes to see doors flying open in front of me. I'm alive but forever changed. I close my eyes again.

The next time I open them, Dad and Charlotte are peering down at me. Rat is there, too, hanging around in the background. His face pops in and out of my line of vision every once in a while.

"How are you feeling, peanut?" The furrowed line between my dad's eyes seems deeper than I remember.

"Not sure," I mumble. "Am I skinny yet?"

They laugh like I've made a very funny joke.

A nurse leans into my line of sight and pushes something into my hand. I can't look down at it because my head is not connected to my body.

"Don't be a hero," she says. "Push the button to get the pain medicine."

I push the button in my hand. It doesn't hurt anywhere yet, but I don't want to feel any pain. My eyes feel heavy, and I close them again. When I open them again, Rat is sitting in a chair over by a window. It's dark outside, and he is reading a book by lamplight.

"What time is it?" I croak out.

He startles. "Hey, you're awake."

He gets out of the chair and comes over to smooth my hair back from my forehead. Even with the fuzziness in my brain, I know that doesn't seem right. Rat's never touched me like that before. It confuses me. I move away from his touch and punch the button in my hand.

"It's about eight. You've been sleeping for a while now." His voice trails off as his eyes meet mine. I blink once — twice — trying to clear my vision. He looks worried, which is a strange look for Rat. "Your dad and Charlotte just went to get something to eat in the cafeteria. They won't be gone long. Are you in any pain?"

"I don't think so." His question reminds me to push the button in my hand again. Probably way too soon, but time is hazy right now and I'm scared.

"The doctor came by earlier. He said everything went great."

"Good," I say. "When can I go home?"

"Probably tomorrow."

"Are you okay?" I ask, because I've never seen that look on his face before. Something between unsure and scared.

"Yeah," he says. "I guess I was just a little worried. It all seemed so rational, until it actually happened. And it was you."

My forehead creases in bewilderment. "But I'm going to be all right." I can't believe I'm trying to make him feel better. Aren't I supposed to be the patient here?

"I made something for you while I was waiting for you to come back to Recovery." He unfolds a piece of paper and holds it over the bed rail so I can see. I lick my cracked lips and try to focus on what he's holding out to me. It's an intricate pencil drawing of a tiny pumpkin. The vine and leaves twist and turn across the page with incredible, almost scientific, detail.

"You did this?" My mouth feels dry, my throat raw. I blink the blurry from my eyes once more and stare down at the tiny picture. I'm amazed. "I never knew you could draw like this."

"It's a pumpkin," he says.

"I can see that," I say, trying to smile. I try to concentrate and understand. Rat did this. For me. Even in my current state, I can see it's remarkable. "Why didn't you ever show me your drawings before?"

"Drawing is different than science or math. It's not measurable." There's a long pause. I give him a weak smile and then he adds, "You might not like it."

"But it's wonderful," I say, taking the paper from him with a shaky hand.

"I was just thinking while you were in surgery. I know how you like fairy tales, but I can't draw fairy godmothers and carriages and stuff like that very well. Not like your mom."

I feel the tears well up in my eyes and one slides slowly down the side of my face onto the hospital pillow. How did he know I was thinking of her?

"What did she say to you that day in the hospital?" I ask.

He knew what I was talking about. She'd asked us all to leave that day except for Rat. I watched through the window as she talked and he took notes carefully, his face too serious for a ten-year-old.

"She told me to take good care of you."

"And that's what has made you stick it . . . me . . . out?"

"I promised," he says, solemnly. "Besides I'm really good at it."

"Yes, you are."

"You know she would be proud of you," he says, brushing my tear away with the tip of his finger. "And she would really want to be here now if she could. So I drew this pumpkin to remind you of that."

"It's an amazing pumpkin," I say, sniffling just a little bit. "Much better than fancy carriages and fairy godmothers."

"Cinderella needed that pumpkin for everything else to happen. Everybody has to start somewhere." Rat folds the drawing up and tucks it under the cup of ice chips on the tray in front of me. "Now you're ready for the magic to happen."

"She needed a Rat, too," I say.

"Doesn't everybody?" he asks with a laugh.

Someone enters the room. I turn my head slowly to see Briella with a backpack and some school books. Quickly, I wipe away the traces of tears from my face with the hand that doesn't have tubes coming out of it. Briella glances at me, but quickly looks away like she's not sure if she wants to see me or not.

"Charlotte dropped me off. She said for me to stay here because Rat needs a break."

Rat steps back from the bed and stretches with a long groan. "I probably should walk around for a bit."

I didn't realize he'd been here all this time. I feel a little guilty.

"You'll be all right for a few minutes without me?" he asks.

"Sure. I brought my English homework," Briella says.

"I think he means me," I say.

"Oh, yeah. Right," she mumbles, slouching down into the chair with her books in her lap.

"I'll be okay," I say to Rat. "Go get something to eat."

He waves to both of us and leaves. Briella looks at me nervously and then down at her books, opening one randomly to a page near the middle.

"Don't worry. I'm not going to die while you're here," I say.

"Good," she says, " 'cause you look really bad."

"Thanks."

"Does it hurt?"

"Not too much. Just feels weird with all these tubes."

"I didn't know," she says, standing up and walking over to the side of my bed.

"Know what?"

"That it would be so . . . hard."

I give a short laugh, but abruptly stop, clutching my stomach at the quick stabbing pain it caused.

"Did you think it would be like going to the dentist or something?" I say.

I don't tell her the hard part is only just now starting. Let her try spending her days eating three tablespoons of food for each meal.

"Why do you always act like I'm so stupid?" Briella asks.

Of course, now it's all about her. Even with me lying in a hospital room stuck full of tubes everywhere. I don't have the energy to argue with her. I punch the button in my hand and lean back on the pillow, closing my eyes.

"You're not stupid," I say in a monotone. Eventually, I hear her move away from the bed and go back to the chair.

"You're lucky you don't have to take finals," Briella says from the chair. "I wish I could miss the last five weeks of school."

"Good grades make a lot of things possible. You should try it," I say, with my eyes still closed. "Besides I think finals would have been a lot easier than this."

"For you, maybe."

I open my eyes and look over at Briella. She has her English book open now, and she is staring down at a blank notebook page, twirling a pencil around in one hand.

"What's your grade?" I ask.

"I don't want to talk about it."

"It can't be that bad. You've paid me to write almost every essay."

"It wasn't all essays. There were some stupid in-class tests over the readings. You couldn't take those for me," she mumbles. "Summer school's bad. Mom is going to kill me."

"Can you save it with your final?" It feels good to talk about something besides the surgery. Something normal outside these hospital walls.

"I could, but I won't. I've never brought my grade up by a final. I'm not so good at tests. Besides, I have this big essay due next week even before finals."

Her shoulders slump, and she looks so dejected I almost take pity on her. Then I remember. It's Briella.

"You didn't come here just to give Rat a break, did you?"

"What do you mean?" She gives me an "I don't know what you're talking about" look, and I know I've nailed it.

"You've got to be kidding, Briella. Look at me," I yell across the hospital room. "You want me to do your homework now?"

"Don't get so excited. It's no big deal. Honestly." Briella rolls her eyes at me and slams her book shut. She scribbles angrily on the paper in front of her.

"She's only glad you're alive because of what you can do for her. She doesn't care about you."

Evidently, Skinny survived the surgery, too.

CHAPTER NINE

Five days after the surgery, someone knocks on my bedroom door.

"Come in."

"Hey." It's Rat, followed closely by Roxanne. She has a yellow tennis ball in her mouth and her tail is whipping around like a helicopter. She loves Rat almost as much as she loves food. Which is saying a lot.

"Aren't you supposed to be in school?" I ask him.

"I called and told them I was going to have the flu this week."

"But you will ruin your perfect attendance record." Rat hasn't missed a day of school since we all had chicken pox in first grade.

"It's okay. Principal Watson has decided not to give out the certificates. He doesn't want to reward kids for doing what they should do." His blond hair is sticking out on the top of his head like he just ran his hands through it. But it always looks like that. "I'm exempt from all my finals anyway."

I always forget about the perfect grade-point combination that results in the exemption prize. I'm usually close, but not perfect. Apparently, the only way I get to skip finals is with a major doctor's excuse and tons of extra work.

Roxanne's brown head pops up over the side of the bed. She has the tennis ball in her mouth and a hopeful look on her face. While I watch she carefully opens her mouth and lets the tennis ball roll across the bed toward my hand. I ignore her.

"So you're here?" I have to admit I like the idea. I breathe in a deep sigh and feel myself relax.

"Somebody had to get you started on the right track." He slides his backpack off his shoulder and perches on the edge of my bed. "Charlotte and your dad had to go back to work. Ugly One and Two are at school. Who else?"

Roxanne jumps up, retrieves the tennis ball lying untouched by my hand, returns to her spot beside the bed, and repeats the whole process all over again. The ball rolls slowly across the bed until it rests beside my fingers. Her face says it all: *PLEEEEASE!* She is stubborn when it comes to playing. I pick up the ball and Roxanne dances back from the bed in happy anticipation. Then I throw the tennis ball out my open bedroom door over the banister, wincing at the sudden unexpected pain of the movement. The ball bounces down the stairs and Roxanne takes off — thrilled. It's so easy to please a Labrador. I hear her thunder down the stairs in glee.

"Charlotte said they were going to hire someone to sit with me during the day," I say.

"Voilà. You're looking at him. Besides, I can use the extra money for a new lens for my telescope."

Roxanne is back at the edge of the bed again. She opens her mouth and lets the ball roll across my comforter toward my hand then sits back and stares at me with huge, pleading brown eyes. *PLEEEEASE!*

"I can't. It hurts," I say to her. She looks totally bummed and lies down on the floor with a big "I'm so disappointed in you" sigh. Guilt. It's another thing Labradors are good at.

"What are they paying you?" I look back at Rat.

"Same thing they pay for Roxanne's day care."

"They're paying you to *dog-sit* me?"

"Want a treat? Sit."

"Very funny."

"Well, I couldn't say *lie down* because you're already doing that." He unzips the backpack and pulls out the all-too-familiar informational booklet. "Now let's see what we're supposed to do today."

I groan.

He starts to read, "There will be white tape known as Steri-Strips on your incision sites. These need to stay on for five days post-op. They should then be removed so the incisions can have open air. Don't worry about the incisions coming apart — there are two layers of dissolving sutures under the Steri-Strips." He leans over the bed. "So, let's see what they look like."

"Really?"

He nods. Before the surgery there was no way I would show anyone my bare stomach. But in the last week, so many people have poked and prodded me, I am sort of getting used to it. Besides, this is Rat, and at the moment he is all I have. I pull up my T-shirt and reveal the two white bandages.

"Humm." Rat inspects the incisions with the interest of a scientist looking through a microscope at the cure for cancer. "Redness around the incision of one-fourth an inch is not unusual. Do they hurt?"

"Just a little sore."

"Good. Some pain at the incisions is normal, but after forty-eight hours it should improve daily. If it becomes more tender after this period, especially if there is increased redness, if swelling has increased, and if there is drainage or bleeding, then there may be infection. At that point we should call the doctor." He recites it all from memory. "We don't need to call the doctor. It's been nearly a week since the surgery, and there's very little redness."

I pull the T-shirt back over the top of my stomach and watch Rat retrieve his laptop out of his backpack. "What's that for?"

"I need to record today's data." He types away at the keyboard. "I'm keeping a chart. Going to print it out and put it right up there on the wall." He motions toward the space beside my bedroom door but doesn't look up from the computer.

"What data?"

"Weight loss. Exercise. Attitude." He looks up expectantly from the screen and announces, "Week two. Weight?"

Again, not something I would ever want anyone to know, but this morning I stepped on the brand-new bathroom scale Charlotte bought me before the surgery, and the news was actually pretty good.

"Two eighty-five," I say.

"Weight loss?"

"Seventeen pounds."

"Right on target." Rat types it into the computer. "Exercise?"

"Since I've been home?" I ask, trying to stall. After all, he'd been there for most of my walks around the hospital hallways, carefully supervising me while I pushed my rolling rack full of connected bags of dripping liquids.

"I mean," he pauses for emphasis, "over the last three days since I've been back in school and you've been here."

"You're looking at it," I finally confess.

Rat glances back up at me and frowns. "That will have to change. Attitude?"

"Grumpy." He types down my response. "I'm hungry. I want to eat something."

"The good news is if you can pour it, you can eat it. According to the doctor's info, if you can suck it through a straw and it's about the consistency of pancake batter, you can have it."

"That's good news?" I ask.

"What did you eat last week?"

"I didn't eat. I drank my meals. Clear liquids."

Rat types away on his computer, mumbling, "Good, good." He pauses and flips through the papers in his hand. "Let's see what's on the menu for week two. Broth, cream soups, diet popsicles, watery grits, oatmeal, or cream of wheat. Then we can start to work in mashed-up foods in weeks three to six."

"Yum," I say, frowning. Six weeks seems like a really long time without chewing.

"Now we work on the attitude and the exercise." Rat closes his computer and stands up. "Come on."

I am still wary the pain will surprise me when I get out of bed, so I move carefully. I push the covers slowly back from my legs. I'm wearing gray stretchy sweats and socks that Charlotte helped me put on before she left for work. I wondered why she was so insistent about helping me get into the clothes and so determined to brush my thick tangled hair up into a ponytail. Now I realize she was trying to make me presentable for the dog-sitter.

Rat reaches behind me to push gently against my back, supporting me, while I sit up slowly. There is an intense, pulling tightness at my stomach, and I stop to breathe in deeply. Once. Twice. The pain pills are working, but I still murmur an "ouch" as I stand, wobbling only slightly.

I shuffle out slowly to the top of the stairs with Rat and Roxanne close behind. Rat holds my elbow and I step gingerly down each step, one at a time. At the bottom, we turn around and I start back up again. Roxanne is thrilled with the new game. She accompanies us every step of the way, ball in mouth. After two very slow trips up and down the stairs, I'm allowed to sit down on the couch.

"And now . . ." Rat picks something up off the coffee table and waves a DVD in front of my face, "your reward."

I've never been a big fan of movie versions of musicals, always preferring the stage, but *Chicago* is about as good as it gets. I smile at Rat and settle back into the cushions of the sofa.

"You put it in, and I'll get us a snack," he says.

He comes back in a few minutes with a bowl of clear brown soup and a sack full of microwaved popcorn. I push PLAY.

My brain says I'm hungry. My hands want to put something in my mouth, but my throat won't accept it. I take a spoonful of soup. I feel like I've just eaten a Thanksgiving dinner. I need to eat more. I take another spoonful. I almost can't swallow it. I push it down my throat. It stops somewhere near the middle of my chest. This can't be it. I have to eat more.

I watch Rat put handfuls of popcorn in his mouth. The smell is incredible. My hands twitch to pick up a handful. What do you do when you watch a movie? You eat popcorn. That's normal. But I'm not normal now. He chews, and I swear I can hear every crunch. I can't hear the dialogue. All I can think of is what popcorn used to taste like. He glances over at me, realizing I'm watching him.

"This bothering you?" He talks around the last handful of popcorn he put in his mouth seconds ago. I don't have to answer him. "Sorry."

He puts the popcorn on the coffee table, and I feel guilty. He shouldn't have to pay for what I can't do anymore.

"It's okay," I say. "I'm going to have to get used to it."

I'm actually starving. My body knows it's consuming itself, my mind knows it, too, but there is nothing I can do about it. I sip the Diet Coke in front of me. I can't take another sip. My throat rejects it. It won't go down. I'm like a cup of water that's completely full. Not a single drop will go in. I'm not sick like throw-up sick. It just won't go into my body. So it comes back up. I run to the bathroom and cough up a small drop of soda into the toilet.

I come out of the bathroom to find Briella in the living room.

"How was school?" Rat asks her.

"Okay, I guess," Briella answers. She kicks off her sandals and walks over barefoot to the popcorn bowl. Scooping up a handful and stuffing it into her mouth, she plops down onto the couch beside Rat. "English is going to kill me."

"Not your best subject?"

"I don't think I have a best subject." Briella frowns. "At least I'm not the only one struggling with English. You should have seen Chance today."

"What happened?" Rat doesn't look at her. Briella pulls out her phone and starts texting.

"He forgot his homework." They both laugh. I don't get the joke.

"What was the excuse this time?" Rat asks.

"He left his bedroom window open last night, and the wind blew it outside. When he tried to climb up the tree to get it back, he fell and sprained his ankle. Spent the rest of the night in the ER."

"Was he limping?"

"Of course. He always has the supporting details right. Even had his ankle all wrapped up."

"Creative," Rat says, smiling broadly.

"Always," Briella agrees, still texting.

"What happened to the paper?"

Hey, I'm watching a movie here. Who knew Rat was suddenly going to turn into Chatty Cathy? I make a huffing sound, but they don't stop.

"Claimed it was still in the tree last time he checked."

I look back and forth at them. They are talking like old friends. When did this happen? I frown and sit back down on my side of the couch. No one pays any attention to me. I stare at the television and watch Renée Zellweger sing "My Own Best Friend," but I don't really hear it.

"He likes her better than you. You think he's your best friend, but it only lasts until someone skinnier and prettier walks into the room." Skinny's voice in my ear is so loud I can't hear the music.

"You're lucky you don't have to go to school, Ever." Briella puts her long tanned legs up on the coffee table and her short blue-jean skirt rides up on her thighs. Rat notices. How could he not?

Funny. I don't feel so lucky right now.

"Did you get your essay back?" Rat asks her.

"Yeah. I made a C."

"Congratulations." Rat gives her a sideways high five.

"If I can pull a B on the final I might get out of summer school."

"I can help you study if you want." He says it so casually; I almost wouldn't know how much he was counting on her response. Almost.

"Sure," she says. Standing up, she swings her hair over her shoulder and heads toward the stairs. "That'd be great."

"I can help you study if you want," I repeat in a snarky voice under my breath.

"What?" Rat looks over at me innocently.

"How can someone so big be so invisible?" Skinny asks.

	Weight	Pounds Lost	Exercise	Playlist
STARTING WEIGHT: 302 HEIGHT: 5'6"				
Week 2	285	17	None	"The Point of No Return" (*The Phantom of the Opera*)
Week 3	275	27	Stairs (2 times daily)	"I Dreamed a Dream" (*Les Misérables*)

Rat and I stare up at the chart he's just finished tacking up on my bedroom wall. It was actually his idea to put the playlist column on the chart. I've always said it'd be great if we could hear the soundtrack of our lives playing in the background. He remembered.

"Isn't that the song the lady from England sang on that reality talent show?" Rat asks. I can see his back muscles working through the thin material of his faded red T-shirt as he writes the words on the chart. When did Rat get muscles?

"What?"

"The song from *Les Misérables*." He points at the chart, and I notice his hands. My hands have always been the only tiny thing about me. If my hand was in his, my fingers would barely reach his knuckles. But it isn't. I blink to clear my head. The lack of calories must be affecting more than just my weight.

"Didn't I hear it on the radio?"

"Unfortunately," I say. "Many people don't even know the song comes from *Les Misérables*, one of the most famous and most performed musicals worldwide. It's the only song that actually made the charts from the musical just because of that woman singing it on *Britain's Got Talent*."

"But it's getting better, right?"

"What do you mean?" I ask.

"Your mood. Last week we were at the point of no return, going into the depths of the opera house, following the phantom, a vicious murderer. If that was any indication of your mind-set, it couldn't have been good. This week we're dreaming a dream. I figure, it's got to be better."

I'm surprised he remembers so much about *The Phantom*. I thought he was reading some physics textbook when I was watching it on DVD. Three times.

"*Les Misérables* is set in nineteenth-century revolutionary France," I say. "'I Dreamed a Dream' is sung by Fantine who had bright hopes for love and life until reality took over, and her life became worse than she had ever imagined. When you actually listen to the words it's all about lost hope."

"Your music choices are depressing," Rat says.

"It's my soundtrack," I say. Yesterday an ad for Burger King came on the TV, and I started to cry. Who cries over a hamburger commercial? I just want to believe someday I can actually eat a hamburger again. I grieve the loss of hamburgers and ice cream and M&M's. Lost hope. What have I done to myself?

"Losing twenty-seven pounds since the surgery is pretty amazing," Rat says, clearly still disappointed in my song choices. He only records the weight once a week, even though he and I both know I'm secretly weighing myself every single day. Sometimes more than once a day. Every day the number on the scale is a little lower than the day before.

I try not to hope too much but I feel a little spark growing somewhere deep inside me every time I see that little marker go down another couple of pounds. I know the weight loss will slow down now, but what if it stops entirely? What if I fail at this, too? This is my last chance.

	Weight	Pounds Lost	Exercise	Playlist
Week 2	285	17	None	"The Point of No Return" (*The Phantom of the Opera*)
Week 3	275	27	Stairs (2 times daily)	"I Dreamed a Dream" (*Les Misérables*)
Week 4	267	35	Stairs (4 times daily)	"Wake Me Up When September Ends" (*American Idiot*)

"Why *American Idiot*? It's not your usual choice for musicals," Rat asks, after he finishes writing down my song for the week on the chart. He flops down on the bedroom floor beside me and pulls out his laptop to update the results.

"Billie Joe Armstrong is the lead singer for Green Day and he also wrote *American Idiot*. I read on his website that he wrote that song for his father, a jazz musician and truck driver, who died of cancer when he was only ten years old." I lean back against my headboard and stretch my legs out on the bedspread in front of me.

"But why is it *your* song for this week?" Rat sits cross-legged on the floor in front of the chart.

"I'm hoping by September everything will be different. School will start. I'll be thinner. Maybe I'll be used to this by then," I say. "Maybe it won't be so hard."

Rat nods, but I know he doesn't understand. Because it *is* hard. Harder than I ever imagined. I knew food is . . . was . . . the center of my world. Now, there is no public or private eating. I can't eat anywhere anymore, and I don't know what to do in its place.

Rat shuts his laptop. "If you're going to be in that musical next year, you're going to have to get out there and exercise. You saw how they performed *Oklahoma*, right? Even high school actors have to move."

"Next week . . ." My voice trails off as his eyes meet mine.

"*Right. Like that's going to happen,*" Skinny says sarcastically in my right ear.

	Weight	Pounds Lost	Exercise	Playlist
STARTING WEIGHT: 302 HEIGHT: 5'6"				
Week 2	285	17	None	"The Point of No Return" (*The Phantom of the Opera*)
Week 3	275	27	Stairs (2 times daily)	"I Dreamed a Dream" (*Les Misérables*)

	Weight	Pounds Lost	Exercise	Playlist
Week 4	267	35	Stairs (4 times daily)	"Wake Me Up When September Ends" (*American Idiot*)
Week 5	263	39	Walk/Run	"Seasons of Love" (*Rent*)

I finish writing the song for the week on the chart and try to ignore the words written in the next column under "Exercise."

"The song is about time passing," I say to Rat, "and about all the things that can change in a year."

"You can't spend all your time waiting," Rat says. "This is the week we get serious about exercise."

I feel a little sweaty and lightheaded when I look at that entry "Walk/Run" on the chart. I'm supposed to run? Really? I don't know what's bothering me more — that I'm going to be expected to go outside and exercise in front of the whole neighborhood or the fact that I only lost four pounds this week. And that feels crazy, since before the surgery I would have been thrilled to lose four pounds in a week. But now it's different. I'm getting used to the big numbers and if it takes exercise to get them again, then that's what I'll do. I've come this far. I'm not going to stop now.

"Let's go eat some lunch and then we'll go for a run," Rat says, like that is the most normal thing in the world. He puts a little smiley face beside the number of pounds I've lost — thirty-nine since the surgery — with a bright green Sharpie marker.

"But, first an experiment." He rubs his hands together and leers like a mad scientist.

"On me?" I ask.

"Not on you, *for* you. Totally different."

"Okay," I say, cautiously.

"Really I guess you would call it a demonstration. About the rules." He bends down to tie his tennis shoe and misses the big grimace on my face.

"I hate all these rules," I say.

"There's a reason for the rules." He stands back up and heads out the door. "You'll see," he says over his shoulder.

I look at the perky little smiley face on the chart, and the number beside it, but I don't feel like smiling about the lunch, the demonstration, or the run. I slowly follow Rat downstairs to the kitchen.

"Come here," he says, from the sink. "What's the worst rule to follow while you're eating? The one you're determined to ignore."

I don't hesitate. "Not drinking anything while I eat," I say.

"Right." He has a paper cup in his hand and, while I watch, he pokes a hole in the bottom with an ink pen. "I'm leaving about an inch hole, which is about the size of the outlet out of your stomach," he says. He pours some water in the cup slowly and it goes right through the hole almost as fast as it went in.

"As I pour faster, it will begin to back up, but as soon as I stop putting in more water, it will empty rapidly." He demonstrates. "That's why gastric bypass patients can usually drink without difficulty."

"That little hole in the bottom of my new little stomach is also why a fizzy Diet Coke doesn't go down so easily anymore," I say.

"Exactly." He beams at me, pushing his glasses back up his nose.

"Next, let's take a soft food." He puts a couple of scoops of leftover mashed potatoes from the fridge in the bottom of the cup. "Notice that the first spoonful stays in the cup, but as you put more in, it forces some out of the outlet. If I put in chopped-up hamburger, steak, or chicken, it will empty very slowly. Shall we try it?"

I can tell he really wants to because Rat really loves a good experiment, but I just say, "No, I believe you."

He frowns at me, but continues, "If you put in a big piece of bread or a large chunk of meat, it won't empty at all."

"Got it," I say.

"Now, here's the interesting part." His eyes start sparkling behind his glasses like it's Christmas. "If I pour water over the top of these mashed potatoes, what happens?"

I watch as the diluted food drips through the hole at the bottom of the cup.

"The cup empties," I say.

"And?" he asks, waiting for it.

"So does my stomach," I say.

"Right!" He shouts it so loud, I jump. "And then you'll be hungry again and you will want to eat more."

"What's going on in here?" Dad stomps his tennis shoes on the back step before he comes in the kitchen door. He's in his mowing-the-lawn Saturday shorts and T-shirt.

"We were just finishing up an experiment," I say, grabbing up the paper cup and dumping it into the garbage beside the sink.

Dad pulls open the freezer door, dislodging a picture of Lindsey doing the splits, holding big green pom-poms over her head. Putting it back on display, he tucks it a bit more securely under one of the watermelon-shaped magnets, then surveys the inside of the freezer with a frown.

"You want to stay for lunch?" he asks Rat. "I'm going to heat up Ever's favorite, spaghetti and meatballs."

"Sure," Rat says. "Need any help?"

"Nope. It'll be ready in a few minutes."

We leave him clattering around, pulling out pans from the cabinet. I know my dad's trying, fixing favorite foods for Saturday lunch and all, but most of the time he looks at me like he's scared to talk about food or dieting or how I look. Like I'll instantly run upstairs to cram chocolate cake in my mouth and gain back all the pounds I've lost. Like it's all so fragile and could disappear with just the wrong look or the wrong words.

So I think I'm slowly shrinking, but it's evidently a big secret. Either that, or I'm not really looking any different at all. I'm not sure.

Charlotte comes in from the backyard carrying a freshly cut bouquet of yellow roses from the yard. Carefully slicing each stem off at the perfect angle, she arranges them symmetrically into a vase, equal spaces apart. Charlotte likes things orderly. Even flowers. The three different bottles of perfume she keeps on the top of her dresser are exactly lined up, even spaces apart, right next to the wooden plaque that reads, GOD ISN'T FINISHED WITH ME YET. There's also a pyramid of large pink Velcro rollers on the dresser top, perfectly stacked, that has something to do with her daily hair routine, but I haven't quite figured that out yet.

After the roses are arranged, Charlotte pulls out the plates and forks to set the table, chattering all the while about, "isn't it nice to have company for lunch." Lindsey gets off the couch and slowly meanders to the table, talking on her phone the whole time. It's rare that we're graced with her presence. Charlotte calls upstairs for Briella, but we don't wait.

"Hang up the phone, please," Dad says, and Lindsey does but I can see she's still texting from her lap.

Sitting at a table filled with food is an exercise in torture. Everything looks good. Everything smells delicious. The spaghetti in front of me is in fact my favorite. Big meatballs drenched in marinara sauce. French bread toasted in the oven with butter. I start to feel nervous. It happens every time now when I'm going to need to make a food choice. Choose the right thing and I might actually feel good, satisfied. Make the wrong choice, which usually happens these days, and I'll be in the bathroom throwing it back up in minutes. I'm supposed to eat the protein first, that's what the doctor told me, but I want the pasta and the bread. My mouth waters to sink my teeth into the doughy goodness of bread. Big, raw, torn-off pieces of hot comfort.

I put a meatball on my plate, a small piece of bread, and a spoonful of pasta. Before the surgery, this would have been a couple of bites, but now it will be my whole meal. I force myself to take a bite of the meatball first. Tiny. The end of a forkful. I chew like crazy and swallow. It goes down, but I want a drink of water. I reach for the glass and then make myself stop. I remember Rat's experiment and that is why, when I'm sitting here chewing away at this tiny bite of meatball and wanting water to drink with it so badly you'd think I was staggering across a desert, I don't pick up the glass in front of me.

One of the rules. Like eat the protein first and don't eat anything sweet. Strange though, it's one of the hardest rules to follow. Now I crave water while I'm eating. I guess you don't miss it until you know you can't have it. I started out deciding it was a stupid rule and I wasn't going to follow it. I mean, after all, I had enough to suffer through at every meal, why would drinking make such a difference?

Briella slides into the chair across from Rat, breaking my focus on the water glass in front of me.

"You're back early," Charlotte says. "I thought you were going to spend the night at your dad's."

"He had things to do," Briella mumbles, stuffing a huge forkful of pasta into her mouth.

"How's the baby?" my dad asks. Charlotte glances over at my father with a quick frown. The new baby is not a popular topic with Briella. Even I know that.

"Just like any other baby," Briella says. "It poops and cries."

The subject is closed. Everyone eats in silence for a while, until finally Charlotte can't stand the awkwardness anymore.

"Lindsey got her roommate assignment today from the University of Kansas," Charlotte announces in her fake perky voice. Lindsey doesn't look up from her lap; her food sits untouched on her plate. I watch Briella drink half a glass of her water and then effortlessly go back to stuffing another forkful of spaghetti into her mouth. "She met her roommate at cheerleader camp and guess what?"

No one guesses. I'm really thirsty. My hand crawls a little closer to the water glass.

"They are both going to major in communications this fall!"

"Yay," Briella says in a monotone.

Just one sip. Not enough to water down the food in my tiny little stomach and drain it out the hole in the bottom. Just a little tiny bit.

Lindsey finally looks up and across the table at her mom. "I need a new bedspread and curtains for the dorm room."

"I don't know, Lindsey." Charlotte looks uncomfortable and

glances at my father. "We already spent a lot on your new computer."

"Whatever," Lindsey says, and goes back to texting.

Charlotte's eyes fill up with hurt, but she blinks it away quickly. I can't help but feel sorry for her.

"Dad says he feels bad he missed the graduation ceremony. Says he's going to call you and take you out for lunch," Briella tells Lindsey, who finally picks up a whole meatball with her fork and takes a big bite off the side.

"Yeah, like we both know that's going to happen," Lindsey mumbles through the meatball.

Charlotte turns her attention to Rat. "What are you doing this afternoon?"

"Ever and I are going for a run," Rat says, like this is completely possible.

I put down the water glass before it makes it to my lips. Gigi is probably dancing her way through the summer. Chance is definitely playing baseball. And Ever is running. Right.

"I could go with you," Briella says, breaking my focus on the water glass. "I like to run."

Really? Are you kidding me? Who *likes* to run?

"Sure," Rat says. I kick him under the table, and he looks over at me with raised eyebrows.

I frown at him, but I can tell by his puzzled expression he has no clue why I'm annoyed. Briella pushes away from the table and heads up the stairs, calling back, "I'll just get my tennis shoes."

Rat and I go outside and wait for her on the front steps. I want to go upstairs and get my iPod. Music blaring in my ears is the only thing I can think of that would make this any better, but the idea of climbing up the stairs is too much trouble. If that's too hard, how am I supposed to run around the block?

"The whole neighborhood's going to love this. They'll probably feel the vibrations in the ground and think it's some kind of earthquake. Hope you don't break the concrete," Skinny says.

"I don't want to do this," I say.

"The first day of school is only a few months away," Rat says. "And then you can try out for the musical. And go to the Fall Ball."

And Jackson will finally see me again, I think, but I don't say anything to Rat about Jackson. I'm not sure why.

"That seems like a long way away," I say. "Besides, what do you know about balls and musicals?"

"Nothing," he says, "but I know a lot about you." He gives me one of his rare Rat smiles, his straight white teeth flashing suddenly in his usually serious face.

I glare back at him. It's already blazing hot. I can feel the sweat rolling down the side of my neck and I'm sitting still. Even Rat is sweating, his forehead beaded with moisture. He stands up suddenly, pulls up the hem of his T-shirt, and wipes his brow off, revealing a tight six-pack of muscles across his stomach. My breath catches in my throat.

He notices me staring. "What?" he asks.

"Have you been working out?" I ask, still staring at his ripped abs.

"Brazilian jujitsu. It's a martial art based on ground fighting. Derived from the Japanese martial art of Kodokan judo in the early twentieth century, it favors leverage over brute strength." He pats his still-exposed stomach with one hand, and I feel my throat go dry. "Great for your core muscles."

Obviously.

"How?" I stammer.

"Over four centuries ago in northern India, Buddhist monks developed a form of fighting that allowed them to subdue opponents without killing them. Eventually it made its way to Japan, where it was improved upon and called jujitsu."

"No, I mean . . ." How did you get to look like that without me knowing? I stop myself from saying that last part — just barely — and try to cover up my confusion. "How did it get to Brazil?"

"Oh that." Rat drops his shirt back down over his stomach, and I let my breath out, not realizing I'd been holding it. He continues enthusiastically, "In the early nineteen hundreds, Japanese judo master Mitsuyo Maeda came to stay with Brazil's Gastão Gracie. Gracie helped Maeda with business in Brazil and Maeda taught Gracie's family judo."

"Okay. Okay. Got it." I hold my hands up, stopping him from continuing. This is the Rat I know. He will go on for hours if I let him.

He stops the informative lecture, but adds one last thing. "You should try it."

"He's seen your stomach. He knows you could never do anything like that," Skinny says.

I'm mortified at the comparison between my bare stomach and his. "I think this is plenty for me right now," I say, pointing to my sneakers.

"All right, but if you change your mind, you can always go with me to my lessons." He sits back down beside me on the step.

In a few minutes, Briella's back, wearing some black Nike shorts and a sleeveless pink tank top. She bends her leg back and reaches down to grab an ankle, stretching it up behind her at an impossible angle.

Rat watches her with his mouth partly open. "You should stretch," he mumbles in my direction.

Seriously? Give me a break.

"Hello," I yell, waving my hand in front of his face. "Remember me? The patient?"

"What?" he asks, blinking back at me.

"Fat girls don't run," Skinny says.

"Okay. Let's go." Briella takes a few prancing, effortless steps forward and backward. I want to hit her.

"We'll start out slow," Rat says. Like there's any other way for me to start?

We all parade down the front sidewalk to the street. I stumble forward into a sort of a trot/walk, Rat and Briella on either side of me. My knees hurt with each jarring step. Every part of my body moves and shakes up and down. I'm out of breath in a few steps, but I try desperately to hide it.

"You are pitiful!"

"I'm thinking we'll just jog to the end of the street and then walk the rest of the way," Rat says.

I nod, but don't speak. I can't.

Briella jogs ahead and then glances back over her shoulder. Obviously surprised at the pace I'm keeping, she slows down and jogs in place until I catch up.

"When do you think you'll start to really notice a difference in your clothes?" Briella asks, but I can't answer. I have to breathe.

"I'm . . ." Gasp, gasp. ". . . not . . ." Gasp, gasp. ". . . sure." The truth is I've already noticed my clothes are not tight anymore. At least I think they're getting looser, but maybe it's all in my imagination.

"I anticipate she will lose approximately one size in clothes per month for at least the first six to seven months," Rat says. He isn't even breathing hard.

"Wow," says Briella.

The end of the street looks so far away. I want to turn back or at least stop, but my legs keep moving. Step after shuddering step, crashing painfully back down to earth over and over again.

"Stop. You can't do this. It'd be easier to quit now." Skinny sounds firm.

I jog forward a few more steps. The corner looks just as far away as when I started. I glance over at Rat. He looks like he's slowed down to a crawl trying to keep pace with me. He's not breathing hard. He's strolling effortlessly.

"I'm thirsty," I say.

"You're right," Rat says. "I should have brought a water bottle. You need to be drinking water every chance you get."

I look at him, hoping that means we'll stop.

"We'll be sure and drink a glass or two when you get back."

Great. I slog on, one bone-shaking step at a time.

"Why can't she drink water when she eats?" Briella asks. I'm surprised Briella has even noticed. Still, she doesn't have to talk about me like I'm not even here.

"I'm . . ." Gasp, gasp. ". . . right beside you." Gasp, gasp. "I can hear you."

Rat ignores me, too. "Sipping liquids with a meal will wash out the pouch, enabling her to eat two to three times as much, particularly with soft foods. It could cut the weight loss in half."

"Interesting," Briella says.

"Who's she fooling? She's never found you interesting in her life."

I give up. Desperately sucking air into my lungs, I stop jogging and shudder to a walk. Briella and Rat slow to my pace.

Mr. Johnson from across the street is trying to teach his daughter Katie how to ride her bike without training wheels. And next door, Mr. and Mrs. Burns are out in their immaculate yard doing some mysterious preparations for the coming summer that involve a wheelbarrow and several shovels. They all look up and watch the three of us slowly walk down the sidewalk. I feel a trickle of sweat on my forehead begin to roll down the side of my cheek; my shirt is a wet blanket against my back. We make a strange trio. Two tall, thin bookends with a huge, sweaty blob in between.

"So what's up with your dad?" Rat asks my stepsister, and I stumble a few steps, then catch my balance again. No one asks Briella about her father. That's a big no-no.

"He's just totally focused on his new wife and new baby."

I glance over quickly at Briella, shocked. She actually answered his question instead of storming off in a huff. "I used to be daddy's little girl, but it looks like I've been replaced by daddy's little boy."

"That sucks." Rat doesn't try to argue with her, and I have to agree. It does suck. "His loss," he murmurs.

"Yeah," says Briella, and she grins at him. I catch the look between them and glance down at my sneakers trudging down the sidewalk. I don't want them looking at each other like that. I don't know why, but I don't.

We slowly pass a yellow house on the corner with overgrown dandelions and a FOR SALE sign in the front yard. It belonged to the Cat Lady, Mrs. Rattenborg. They found her two weeks after she slipped in the bath and died from hitting her head on the Siamese-cat-shaped soap dish. The animal control people were taking crates of cats away for days. I think the moral of the story is, if you're going to wind up in life with only cats for friends, you should teach them to dial 911.

"Today, let's go around the block. We'll jog as far as you can, then walk the rest of the way," Rat says to me. "Maybe you can jog the whole way by week six"

"I've already jogged as far as I can," I whine. "Besides I thought we were just going to the corner."

"Surprise," Rat says with a grin.

My neighbor Mrs. Decker drives by in a blue minivan. Her kids stare out the window at us. Rat waves, and they wave back.

"They're laughing at you. Look at that fat girl out exercising. Hopeless." Skinny isn't out of breath. Her voice is just as steady as always.

"We should stop at the corner. This is my first day out." I get the sentence out and take a couple more gasps of air. I can't even walk and talk at the same time, much less jog.

"You should exercise at least ten minutes every day this week. By my calculations, ten minutes will take us around the block." Rat is immensely stubborn, but now that I know he's measuring by time, not distance, I slow down even more.

"I'm not sure your calculations are right. It's taking me a pretty long time just to get to the corner."

"You doubt my calculations?" He honestly sounds amazed. "Five minutes to the corner. Tops. Plenty of time to walk the rest of the block."

"What about Lindsey?" Rat asks Briella, and they go back to ignoring me dying beside them. "Are you going to miss her?"

"Maybe I will at first, but in my mind Lindsey's been gone a long time," Briella says. "We haven't been close for" — she pretends to count on one hand — "years, I guess. We're really different."

That surprises me. I always sort of lumped Lindsey and Briella together. Yes, they look different, but they are both perfectly beautiful. And both perfectly oblivious to me. My hair is a wet mess of sweat stuck to my hot head. The sun is so hot that the air feels like it's scalding the inside of my throat.

A group of boys rides by on their bikes. I can hear them coming. I glance back over my shoulder.

"Here it comes."

One of them yells back over his shoulder, "Like that's going to help, lardbutt!" Their laughter floats back to us.

Briella takes off, running after them. Rat and I stumble to a stop and watch in amazement. One of the laughing boys looks back over his shoulder then shouts an alarm to his friends. They start pedaling faster, all laughter gone. It's too late. Briella reaches the one closest to her and kicks the back tire with a force that sends the bike wobbling off toward the curb.

"You big chicken," she yells at him.

"You're crazy!" the guy on the bike yells. He gets his balance back, and rushes to catch up with his friends, who are now laughing at him.

"Yeah, and you're scared of me!" Briella shouts back. She stops in the middle of the street, with both hands on her hips, breathing hard for the first time since we started. When Rat and I catch up, she grins at us in triumph.

"Why did you do that?" I ask in amazement.

"Wow," Rat says. He looks at her like she's Princess Leia or something.

Briella laughs. "They were idiots." She slowly jogs around us in a circle, her cheeks flushed bright pink. "Come on, Ever. One more block to go."

I'm confused. Did she do this for me or for that superhero-worship look on Rat's face? Either way, all this drama means I can at least stagger my way to the end of the block at my own pace.

"It doesn't matter what you do. It will never stop," Skinny chuckles in my ear.

CHAPTER ELEVEN

W hat are you and Whitney doing today?" Dad asks Briella.

Whitney Stone, Briella's newest BFF, leans against the kitchen counter in an ultra-fitted floral tank dress, tapping her French-manicured fingernails impatiently on the marble top. At first, I was convinced she was hanging around Briella to get closer to Lindsey and the cheerleading squad, but now I'm not so sure. Evidently they bonded over a shared love of all things not Shakespeare in their freshman English class. Lucky me.

Dad looks like he's drinking a cup of coffee and reading the paper at the table. Really, he's supervising me eating, or trying to eat, breakfast. I have a plate of scrambled eggs in front of me, and I'm taking tiny, careful bites. Chew. Chew. Chew. I don't want it coming back up. Dad glances up every time I swallow, then quickly looks back at the paper to try and hide the fact that he's watching.

"Going to the mall. I have some money for school clothes. You know, child support." Briella grimaces. Her dad always gives her a lot of money right before school starts every fall. Usually, he also makes a big date with her to take her out to lunch and give it to her in person. Then he cancels it and a big check arrives in the mail a couple of days later. I wouldn't want to choose between my dad and a pair of colorful beaded sandals and a vintage studded bag, but it seems to work for Briella.

"We'll definitely be gone all day," says Whitney. I knew Whitney and Briella were friends, but having her in my kitchen on a Saturday morning is completely intimidating. One of the popular crowd, she dates that cute, six-foot-tall basketball player, Matt Lucero. She's never actually said more than a few sentences to me before, and then only when absolutely necessary. Mostly she just looks at me as though I'm one of those huge Texas tree roaches that scatter across the garage floor when you turn the lights on. So I just sit in silence, trying to fly under the popular-crowd radar, and concentrate on the dreaded food in front of me. Bite by bite by bite.

"You want some breakfast?" Dad asks Whitney.

I know what she's going to say. Wait for it.

"No, thanks. I'm dieting."

Bingo.

Whitney wears a size zero and I know because she tries to work it into every possible conversation. It's the only time when being nothing is a really big deal.

"Hurry up. The mall is waiting." Whitney rubs her hands together in anticipation and grins. "Thank God for guilty fathers. Briella is a very expensive child to support. It's going to take at least a day to spend all that money."

My dad clears his throat uncomfortably, but he doesn't say anything. It must be hard being a stepfather sometimes.

"The eggs are good," I say, smiling at him. Chew. Chew. Chew.

Whitney is the fashionista of Huntsville High School. She always wears the latest and best. Lucky for her, she not only wears it well, but she can afford it. Her mom's a lawyer and her father is a big plastic surgeon in town. He caused quite a stir when we were in third grade at Shady Grove Elementary School and brought along saline breast implants as props for Career Day. Some kids thought they were water balloons until he did a demonstration on the Reading Center puppet. He was never asked back. Maybe that was his point.

Wannabes stalk Whitney through the high school halls. If she wears patterned purple hose with a plaid skirt one day, the next day there's always at least three more purple-patterned, plaid-skirt-wearing freshmen at school. I swear she could wear a big chicken costume one day and the whole school would be clucking around behind her within a week.

"There's the cutest pair of brown leather riding boots in the window of Charli's. I want to be sure and try those on." Briella shoves a last bit of toast into her mouth and pushes back from the table. "I need them."

I've seen Briella's closet. She doesn't need any clothes . . . or shoes . . . or purses. Whatever.

Another tiny bite. Chew. Chew. Chew. Swallow. Wait and see if I throw up. Dad glances up from the paper.

"Why don't you take Ever with you?" my dad asks. I look up, startled. How did I get pulled into this? "She really needs some new clothes. All of hers are too big."

Briella's mouth falls open, and I stop chewing mid-bite. We both look over at Whitney, waiting to see how she answers.

"How embarrassing would that be? She has to come up with an excuse," Skinny says.

"Good idea." Briella and I both stare at Whitney. "It'll be sort of like those makeover shows on TV."

"Here's my credit card," Dad says, and pulls it from his wallet. "Have fun."

I'm stuck. I can't even think of a good excuse. Rat is working on some kind of computer system upgrade at the community center all day, so even he can't save me now. The truth is I do need some clothes. School starts next week, and everything in my closet is too big now. What used to be the waist of my jeans now slides down over my hips, and I end up waddling around with the crotch halfway down my thighs, feeling like a toddler wearing tights three sizes too small. I just never intended to have an audience present when I went looking for my new size. Especially not an audience that includes Whitney Stone.

Still, there's not much I can do now but take the credit card, pull up my baggy jeans for the tenth time today, and squeeze myself into the backseat of Whitney's white Accord.

Briella and Whitney talk in the front seat as though I'm not there. That's okay. I bite my lip, worrying about how I'm going to ditch the two of them when we get to the mall. It can't be too hard. After all, Briella and Whitney have a huge mall, with a ton of stores full of clothes in their exact tiny sizes, to browse through. They just can't discover that I have to do all my shopping in one tiny corner upstairs at Macy's where all the clothes come in giant sizes and look like something your grandmother would wear.

"You think they don't know that?" Skinny asks.

When we park I jump out of the car.

"So where do you want to meet?" I ask, ready to put the plan into action.

"Oh, no you don't. You're not going anywhere. I've always wanted to do one of those makeovers, and you're my perfect first client. You're coming with us." Whitney links her arm through mine, to both Briella's and my shock. "Did I ever tell you I want to be a stylist?"

"No," I say, anxiety making my hands sweat as Whitney drags me through the door of Macy's and heads to the first section of clothes. Briella lags behind, but follows eventually.

"All the movie stars have stylists." She starts flipping through racks of clothes in the first section right inside the door. She picks out two tops and then moves quickly to the next rack. "Hummmm . . . this might work. And this . . . I don't know about this one . . . but we'll try it."

Briella and I trail her in a daze.

"Here, take these." Whitney hands me an armful of clothes. I don't know how to tell her I need to go upstairs to the fat-people section.

"I don't think they will fit," I try to tell her, but she pushes me into the changing room and closes the door with a snap.

"I'll be next door trying on these skinny jeans. But I want to see these on you. Come on, Briella." I don't hear my stepsister's response.

I'm left staring at the stack of clothes on the chair. What do I do? I can't go out wearing any of this stuff. It's from the regular-size section. I can't possibly fit into any of these clothes. I pick up the first shirt off the top of the pile. It's a baby-doll style. Tiny pink flowers. XL. Not very fitted. Maybe I should just try it. I pull my old faded T-shirt off the top of my head and pull the top on. Surprisingly, it goes over my stomach and down my hips without stopping. I've been avoiding the mirror in the room. I always avoid the mirrors. But I'm going to have to look. Slowly, slowly, I turn and raise my eyes to the mirror. The girl staring back at me looks surprised.

The shirt looks okay. Better than okay. It looks good. I jump up and down. The girl in the mirror jumps up and down. I put my two pinkie fingers in my mouth and pull my lips to the sides in a big crazy face. The girl in the mirror does the same. Oh my God. She's me.

The girl in the mirror gives me a weird look. Last May, she would have never been able to wear this shirt. But it's almost August now and things have changed. She has . . . I have . . . changed. I hold my arms out and twirl around once, almost losing my balance when I hit the chair in the dressing room.

The shirt floats around my body and lands in a smooth curtain of tiny flowers around my hips.

The door pulls open without warning, and I jump. It's Whitney.

"Let's see." She scrutinizes me for a second. "Yeah, that one's okay. Try on the jeans with it. Might work. They're sixteens, but they have some stretch in them. I think they'll fit."

She stands there like she's going to watch me or something.

"Shut the door," I say.

"Okay. But promise me you'll come out when you put the jeans on."

"If they fit." How could they?

I pull the jeans on. They are tight, but they zip. I can't believe it. I'm wearing jeans. From the regular-size department.

"I'm a regular size," I whisper. I can't stop smiling and smiling and smiling at the me in the mirror.

"Are you coming out?"

I open the door and come out slowly.

"Wow," Briella says, her mouth hanging open, her hands full of hangers and clothes.

"Now we can really tell how much weight you've lost," says Whitney. "I told you they would fit. I'm good at this stuff."

And surprisingly, she is. I try on several more tops, and they all fit. Then Whitney helps me pick which two are the best.

"This is only the beginning," she assures me. "You don't want to have everything from one place."

I've never had choices before. I buy the jeans, too, and they are all wrapped up and put into a bag with little string handles.

Whitney insists on accessorizing the outfits with earrings and a chunky necklace. A couple of bras, a pair of cute platform sandals, and three small packages later, I find myself sitting in a tall chair before the Stila makeup counter.

"What's up, Whitney?" the girl with the heavy black eyeliner asks. "What are we doing with your friend here?"

Neither one of them asks me. I guess it's pretty obvious I don't know what I need.

"I'm thinking like a total makeover. Natural, but definitely needs the works."

Whitney and the girl both stare at me.

"You've never worn makeup before?" the girl asks.

"Not really." Most of my experience with makeup has involved Halloween, and I didn't think the Stila girl would be impressed by my use of eyeliner for my Batgirl costume in the fifth grade.

"So we'll start with the basics." She talks to me and applies various creams, powders, and potions. I nod and try to remember it all. Briella and Whitney hover at first, but then wander off to other perfume and makeup counters, leaving me alone with Eyeliner Girl.

"You have great green eyes. Let's try to really make them pop with this deep violet shadow."

I nod like I know what she's talking about, but then when she finally turns me toward the mirror, I see exactly what she means. My eyes look huge.

"Now just a little blush. You need one with rounded bristles like this." She holds a fluffy brush up in front of my face and I nod. "Start at your forehead where the sun naturally grazes your face. Circle down around your temples and along your cheekbones. Blend into the apples of your cheeks. See?"

Who knew I had dimples when I smiled? And my face, with those newly defined cheekbones, looks . . . almost good. I blink and the eyes in the mirror blink back at me.

"She'll take it all." Whitney is back by my side and sharing the reflection in the mirror with me. "Give her the credit card," she says to me.

Eyeliner Girl puts everything into a bag for me. "You really look amazing," she says. "If you have any questions, I'm here every Saturday."

"Time for lunch," Whitney announces, as we leave the makeup counter and head out into the mall. "I'm starved."

We wait in line at California Pizza Kitchen with lots of tired-looking moms and screaming kids. My arms are full of bags from the shopping trip. Clothes, makeup, jewelry, and shoes. I'm afraid of what Dad will say when he sees his credit card statement. Whitney has very expensive tastes. I figure I'll just remind him of the years and years of shopping I've saved him.

I glance up at the restaurant window. There are three girls reflected there. I recognize Whitney and Briella. But who is the third? She has her arms full of colorful sacks and bags — Nordstrom, H&M, Urban Outfitters, Gap. I know it's me, but the girl in the reflection doesn't look like me. I move the bags in my arms up and down. The reflection does the same. It is me. I know it in my head, but the reflection lies. It has to, because the girl in the window is not that fat. She's not skinny, or anything like that, but she's not terrible looking. She has a smile on her face and, if I saw her walking around the mall, I wouldn't feel sorry for her.

"Wait. Look how much fatter you are than the two of them. You're the charity case here, and don't ever forget it."

Skinny is right. I look at the reflection closer. I am fatter than Briella and Whitney. Of course I am.

The hostess starts to seat us. I'm worried when she leads us toward the booths. I won't fit. I can't tell them that I need a table, not a booth. Briella slides in one side and Whitney follows, taking the menus and chatting the whole time. I can't hear them. I'm focused on the space in between the table and the seat. It's too small. I stand there awkwardly.

"Sit down, Ever," Briella says impatiently. "What's wrong?"

"Nothing," I say. I sit gingerly on the bench and push myself into my side of the booth, taking a deep breath. There is room to spare between me and the table. Just a small space left over, but it's there. I fit. I can't celebrate too much, though, because the waitress is here to hand me a menu, and I realize I have an even bigger problem in front of me. What can I eat?

Briella is texting. Whitney is talking. I stare at the menu. All these choices.

"Did you see that Marc Jacobs top? It would look amazing on me," Whitney says.

"Wolfgang just texted me," Briella squeals.

"What did he say?"

Briella hands over her phone, and Whitney reads.

"You don't exist," Skinny reminds me.

I have bigger problems at the moment. The waitress is back, and it's time to order. Whitney and Briella decide to share a pizza, then it's my turn. I order a chopped chicken salad. It seems like the best choice.

The food comes. Briella and Whitney dive into the pizza. I take a tiny bite of lettuce and chew like crazy.

"Your eye shadow looks great." Whitney focuses on me between bites. Briella texts Wolf back about meeting up with him later at the movies.

"Thanks," I say. I take a bite of chicken, smiling. We could be friends.

"Don't kid yourself, fatty."

The chicken stops halfway down my throat. My chest aches with the pressure. I didn't chew it long enough. It's going to come back up.

"I'm thinking that bracelet from Forever 21 would be perfect with that top. What do you think?" I realize suddenly that Whitney's talking to me, not Briella. She's actually asking my opinion. I take a sip of water and nod. The bite of chicken doesn't budge. It feels like an elephant is sitting on my chest. The pressure is painful. I'm afraid I'm going to spew it out across the table.

"I have to go to the bathroom," I say. Whitney is still talking when I leave the table, but all I can think about is getting to the toilet before I hurl. I try not to run. A mom with a toddler is in front of the sink when I push open the door. Luckily, one of the stalls is empty. I barely shut the door before I'm coughing over the toilet. The piece of chicken comes up. Instantly, I feel better.

"Are you all right?" The woman at the sink looks concerned as I step out of the stall.

"I'm fine." I rinse my mouth out at the sink. I don't want to explain. She shakes her head and leaves.

Back at the table, I stare down at the chicken salad. It looks delicious, but I can't have another bite. I know it won't go down, and I don't want to answer the questions I'll get if I run back to the bathroom again.

The waitress returns, looking down at the barely touched salad with a frown. "Is something wrong with your lunch? You don't like it?"

"It's fine," I say.

Briella takes the last bite of the deep-dish pizza and says, "She can't eat that much."

The waitress looks surprised.

"She's shocked. Look at you. Nobody your size eats that little."

"Do you want a box or something?"

I can't eat it now or later. "No," I say and watch sadly as she takes it away. I'm so hungry.

"So are we meeting Wolf later?" Whitney asks, and Briella nods excitedly. They talk about what they're going to wear. Neither of them asks me to go with them, but I didn't expect it.

We split the bill. A waste of money. I scoop up all the bags and follow Whitney and Briella out of the restaurant, noticing the chewing, the smells, and the food everywhere I turn. I'm starving in plain sight, and no one has a clue except maybe the woman in the bathroom who thinks I have an eating disorder. I do. A surgically induced one.

"You'll always be an outsider. Fat and hungry. How does that makeover feel now, stupid?"

On the way home I tune out the noise in the front seat, staring out the side window but not really seeing anything. I feel confused. The shopping felt good. Lunch was horrible. How can I balance the two? Everything revolves around food. Even shopping. I have to admit buying the clothes in the bags next to me gave me a satisfied feeling. It was almost as good as handfuls of M&M's. Almost.

That night, I sit in the middle of the bed with all my new purchases spread out around me, surprised by the strange feelings of excitement at the thought of new starts and a new year. For the first time, I really think about going back to school. I wonder if Gigi will have a new hair color and if Chance will notice my weight loss.

Scattered brushes, eye shadows, and liners have taken new spots on the top of my dresser. And in the midst of all this craziness sits something even more alien — even more intimidating — a long-fought enemy known to inspire dread and despair. A newly purchased handheld mirror.

I peek into it quickly, then stare at the blank line of my weight-loss chart for this week. It's like a big blinking cursor on a computer screen — waiting, waiting, waiting — for me to fill it in. I finally slide off the bed and walk over to pick up a red marker off my desk. In the musical *West Side Story*, there's a song that Maria, the main character, sings in front of the mirror before she goes to the big dance. I write the title of the song on the chart under the column for my playlist and immediately want to scratch it out again. I make myself step away from the chart, leaving the printed words behind.

STARTING WEIGHT: 302			HEIGHT: 5'6"	
	Weight	Pounds Lost	Exercise	Playlist
Week 15	234	68	Run/Walk (1 mile)	"I Feel Pretty" (*West Side Story*)

CHAPTER TWELVE

It's the first day of school. When I enter first-period history, I only glance up long enough to get my bearings. That's surprisingly difficult in this particular classroom. Mr. Landmann, my new history teacher, is also very active in the Huntsville Community Theater and is a requested favorite with students. He somehow combines his two passions, history and theater, in his classroom and it's crammed full of every kind of historical theatrical prop imaginable. I push down the aisle between a gold spray-painted Henry VIII throne and a life-sized cutout of Magellan. I'm looking for a seat in the back as usual. Not trying to draw attention to myself. Some of the seats are already full. People are talking and chatting. New clothes. New haircuts. New hopes for new starts. One girl playfully shoves a boy. I dodge.

I make it to an empty desk in the back corner. One wall behind me. One wall beside me. It feels comfortable. Protected.

The tension from a sleepless night full of first-day-back-at-school nightmares begins to ease up a bit. I pull the desktop up and snap it into place. There's space between my stomach and the desk. I fit. Mr. Landmann is calling roll, and I almost miss my name. I fit.

"Here," I say. I scoot around in the desk. There is room to move. To breathe. I stare at my bare forearms on the desk. It's like someone put the wrong arms on my body. Overnight. They don't look like me. Arms that don't look huge and puffy. They just look like arms. Whose arms are these? My eyes fill with tears, and I feel really stupid for reacting like this. It's just a desk. Everyone else can sit in the desks, too. Why not me?

The bell rings and Mr. Landmann begins lecturing on Tudor England, waving a large papier-mâché sword around wildly. It's one way to keep teenagers' attention first thing in the morning. He climbs on top of his desk, wielding the sword, and accidently knocks a stuffed owl off his bookshelf. The now flying owl wakes up the boys who are sitting in the replica of the *Santa Maria* when it bounces off the mast and lands in their laps.

The lecture comes to an abrupt halt while Mr. Landmann recovers the owl, and I hear a voice beside me.

"Ever, right?" I look over at Wolfgang. He's wearing a camouflage baseball hat that reads, DON'T MESS WITH TEXAS.

"Yes," I say. I can't remember him actually speaking to me before.

"You look different. Did you get your hair cut or something?"

Right. I got a seventy-two-pound haircut. "Or something," I say.

"It's not like you look all that different than before. People can't even tell you lost weight."

I spend most of history looking at my arms. I move them slightly back and forth on my desk and watch them respond to my thoughts. I flex my fingers. They really are my arms.

I glance up at one point and see Jackson looking at me. I look back down, wait a few minutes, and then look back up again. I do this three more times. He's always looking at me. The first two times, he glances away quickly when I meet his eyes. But by the fourth time, he keeps looking at me. Maybe my hair is messed up or something, I think. I smooth the right side of my hair down and tuck it behind my ear. There. He still doesn't look away. Instead, he smiles. I wonder if he means it for someone else, but there's nothing behind me but a wall. I'm supposed to be invisible when I'm just sitting still like this, so what's happening?

I smile back, feeling fizzy bubbles of excitement start to explode in my tiny new stomach. Sudden heat causes my face to flush. It's working. Jackson's looking at me. Noticing me.

First period is over. I collect my notebook and stuff it into my backpack while the front of the class hits the hallway. I'm in no hurry. My next class is just down the hall. English. I'm the last person out the door. The hall is crowded. I keep to one side, with my head down, glancing up only when I need to avoid a direct collision.

A boy with a red baseball hat bumps into me.

"Sorry," I say, even though it's his fault.

"Hey, Ever." I look up to find Whitney and Kristen standing in front of me. Whitney's actually speaking to me. At school. "You look fantastic."

I stand there silent and awkward. I'm not used to compliments.

"Or maybe I should say I made you look fantastic." She punches Kristen on the shoulder, setting all her natural curls bobbing wildly, and says, "I told you. It's my best work yet."

"Ummm . . . thanks," I say. "It's definitely all about you, Whitney."

Oblivious to sarcasm, she nods in enthusiastic agreement.

"I like the DKNY jacket with the jeans. Good touch," Kristen says. They are talking about me as though I'm not here. "And the earrings elongate her face."

"Urban Outfitters," Whitney responds. "I thought they'd go well with that Michael Kors top."

"You were so right."

"I would have suggested boots with it. But her calves just aren't quite ready yet."

"Umm . . ." Kristen looks toward my feet and nods appreciatively. "No, she needs the long lines. Boot cut was a good choice, though."

"I thought so." Whitney leans forward to pick up a handful of my long dark hair. "I'm thinking this will be next. Maybe some bangs? Or layers."

"Highlights at the very least."

Briella walks up to catch the end of the conversation, but when she sees me, her smile freezes on her face.

"Are we going or not?" she asks her friends. "I don't want to be late for history. Mr. Watson will make you pay the whole rest of the semester if you're late."

"In a minute." Whitney waves her off. "I'm showing Kristen my fantastic work on your sister."

"It's pretty amazing," says Kristen.

"Yeah. Fantastic," Briella says. "Now can we go?"

"Excuse me?" Whitney stares at her like she's lost her mind. "Since when have you ever been eager to get to class?"

"I just saw Matt in first period. He said he and Wolf are going to Jilly's after school today. We're going to be there, right?" Briella asks.

Jilly's is a hangout for all the cool kids after school. I've never been, but I know the name.

"Why don't we take . . . umm . . . what's your name again?" Kristen asks me.

"Ever," I mumble. She knows my name. Teachers have been calling it out on the roll of our shared classes for the last three years.

"Great idea. We'll take Ever," says Whitney, clapping her hands together like a five-year-old. "I can't wait to show Maddie Gonzales those earrings I picked out. I just wish we'd taken some before pictures."

I look at Briella's face, and Skinny is quick to tell me her thoughts.

"You're a freak. She doesn't want you to go. You're not good enough to hang out with her friends."

"I can't go," I say. "I have an after-school project. Maybe some other time."

Briella looks relieved. She hooks her arm in Whitney's and pulls her away.

"Maybe some other time," Briella calls out over her shoulder.

I stand there for a few minutes watching them leave, their laughter floating back to me. The hallway is emptying out around me, and I'm suddenly reminded the tardy bell is only minutes away. Books. I still need books for my next class. I step over to my locker and spin the combination, still distracted by what just happened.

"Ever?"

I look up to see Jackson standing beside the lockers. His look is intense and I can see right through the blue in his eyes to the deep green centers. I feel gloriously, deliriously awash in his attention.

"How's it going?" I try to sound natural.

"You sound like an idiot."

"Good. How's your first day?" he asks.

"Good."

"Can't you speak? No wonder he never talks to you anymore. Not worth the trouble."

"So Ms. Lynham was talking in science today about asteroids and meteors and stuff like that." He blurts it out quick and all in one breath. "And then I thought about that time

Rat got that new telescope and we were going to stay up and watch the meteor shower from your backyard. Do you remember that?"

"Yes," I say. "Of course I do." I can barely get it out I'm so astonished he's speaking to me. I'm even more amazed at what he's saying.

"Your mom made up that big pallet of blankets and blow-up air mattresses on the grass."

"She was always up for our adventures," I say. "She went out and bought that outdoor fire pit from Walmart just so we could make s'mores that night while we were waiting for the meteor shower to start. It was a wonder we didn't burn down the deck."

Mom always thought a good time was only made better by food. There's a moment of awkward silence and I realize he must have seen something unguarded in my expression.

"I'm sorry," he says. "About your mom. She was always so funny and nice and all."

"Thanks." There's another beat of quiet.

"Rat was the only one that saw any meteors that night. You and I both ended up sleeping on my couch in the den, remember?" I say into the sudden silence. I don't want the good remembering to be swept away by unexpectedly summoned grief.

He laughs. "Yeah, Rat was always . . ." He searches for the word, tapping his forehead with his index finger.

"Special? Stubborn? Crazy?" I have a million words for Rat.

"I was going to say brilliant."

"That, too." I smile at him. And he smiles back, those blue-green eyes I know so well crinkling up at the corners, and everything is great. Until Gigi Retodo walks by and he nods hello as she passes. His eyes follow her for a minute. I want to grab his shoulders and shake him back into focus. On me.

"Look how much prettier she is than you," Skinny whispers.

I feel my throat tighten and I must make a noise, some kind of sigh or a cough, to strangle the surge of jealousy. Then he does look back at me. For a moment.

"By the way, you look great," Jackson says, and he runs a quick hand through his rumpled, tousled brown hair.

"Umm . . . thanks," I stammer.

"I just wanted you to know." He shifts from one foot to the other. I'm not sure what to say, so I don't say anything. I just look at him. "Well, I guess that's it. See you around?"

I nod, still not really knowing how to respond. Jackson is here. In front of me. Talking to me. Complimenting me. It's like being on a tightrope stretched tautly between two skyscrapers — the past and the future. If I say the wrong thing now, it will be all over. I'll fall and never see the rest of my life with Jackson.

"Of course, it wouldn't be that hard to look better than you did before. You were huge."

"Well, I better go." He turns and walks away in the direction that Gigi went.

I stand there, still not saying a word, wobbling frantically on the tiny wire, afraid to take a step. I don't come to life until he disappears out the double doors at the end of the hall. I pull open my locker door in frustration, and it clangs against the side of the wall over the water fountain. Why didn't I say something?

"Stupid. Stupid. Stupid."

"You like him." Whitney is suddenly standing beside my locker, her eyes narrowed in speculation.

I feel the heat rise up my neck and explode into my cheeks.

"I don't know what you're talking about," I say, pulling my English book out of the bottom of the stack and slamming the door shut.

"Jackson Barnett. You like him. Very interesting."

"Very funny is what she means," Skinny breathes in my ear. *"He's way out of your league. You know it and she knows it, too."*

"Whitney!" Briella yells from down the hall. I'm grateful for the interruption. "Are you coming or not?"

"Just wait a sec," Whitney yells back. She shoves a blue scarf into my hands. "Wear this tomorrow with the flowered shirt. If you need help tying it, see me before school."

Without another word she runs off down the hall to meet Briella. They link arms, giggling, and disappear out the door.

I yank open my locker again and throw the stupid scarf inside.

"Like that's going to help. Now you'll just be a huge blob of lard with a pretty blue scarf tied around it."

I smash the locker door shut and lower my forehead down to the cool metal.

"Somebody's not having such a good day." Rat stands by the water fountain, watching my little temper tantrum. He wears a faded red T-shirt that says COCA-COLA on it and blue jeans. He looks solid and real. "The new look isn't a success?"

"It's going fine."

"That's a sarcastic response, right?"

"People say I look different."

"You do look different."

"But I don't feel any different," I say, wrapping my arms around my books and leaning back against the locker. "On the inside."

"Here," Rat says, with a flash of a brilliant Rat grin. He hands me a flyer on green paper. "This might help."

I look down at the black-and-white drawing of a princess. Beneath the picture are the big, blocky typed words:

TRYOUTS FOR THE FALL MUSICAL: RODGERS AND HAMMERSTEIN'S *CINDERELLA*!

They're going to put on *Cinderella*. I feel a flutter of excitement in my chest. It's my dream role. I know every song, every line by heart. I can recite every bit of dialogue, and every part in the play, from memory. I could blow everyone away, even Jackson, by taking center stage and singing the role of Cinderella. One performance, one night, and no one would ever feel sorry for me again. But then Rat knows that. He's been the only one listening.

It's perfect. So why does that green piece of paper in his hand terrify me?

"What am I supposed to do with this?" I demand.

His smile falters for a moment, but then he continues, "This is what we've been working for, right?"

"I can't. Are you crazy?"

"Why not?" he asks. "What's stopping you? You have to sign up for drama class, but you still have time to change your schedule."

"It's impossible. Crazy. You won't get it. Everyone knows that."

She's stopping me. Skinny. Because I'm wanting something. I'm hoping. I've learned the hard way, hoping is never a good thing. It's all Rat's fault. He caused this.

"Stop pushing me. You're always trying to control everything."

"I just thought you would like it." He's watching me, puzzled.

"That's your problem, Rat. You think way too much about me." I shove him out of the way and head down the hall toward my next class. I don't look back. I don't want to see the hurt on his face, but it doesn't stop me from shouting one last thing back over my shoulder. "Why don't you do a little make-over project on yourself for a change? You'd be the perfect experiment. But wait, they don't have surgery to fix geeks, do they?"

I ignore the openmouthed stares of the two freshmen standing outside the counselor's office. Guilt sears instantly through my brain, but I don't stop walking away. I don't know what I like and don't like anymore. I used to like M&M's and eating.

I used to like Jackson. I didn't like Briella's friends. Now everything feels topsy-turvy.

"You're a freak."

I catch my reflection in the glass doors as I walk past the library. I don't recognize her.

"Good job, fatty. Now everyone hates you."

If I could I would drown my guilt in a huge bag of M&M's, but now I don't know what to do with the bad. I can't eat it away anymore.

CHAPTER THIRTEEN

I've always hated lunch in the school cafeteria. Not only is a fat girl eating a great opportunity for hilarious comments, but living through the hierarchy of where to sit every single day is just torture. It's like walking a gauntlet that, in my case, usually leads to a table over by the trash cans with a bunch of science geeks and other misfits.

This morning, I was so busy trying to pick out the right outfit that I totally forgot my lunch. Now, I'm standing in the lunch line, too overwhelmed to really think about what I can and can't eat. It's too fast. I need more time. Can I eat chicken nuggets? Maybe. If I chew really well. Mashed potatoes. Yes. But I can't fill up on them — no protein. I have to eat protein first. No gravy. Applesauce?

"Does the applesauce have sugar in it?" I ask Hairnet Lady.

"Huh?" She looks at me like I have two heads.

"Never mind," I say. She plops a spoonful of rosy applesauce onto the tray.

When I come out the door into the crowded cafeteria, I search for Rat. If he's here, he'll probably be at the non-popular tables over by the wall. I want to say I'm sorry. The last two hours of class were endless. All I could think of was how horrible I was to him. He didn't deserve it.

"Ever!"

I turn to see Whitney waving frantically from the popular tables by the windows. You've got to be kidding me. But there's no mistaking it. She's waving me over.

"Here. Sit with us." She pushes a frowning Briella down the table and pats the now empty space on the tabletop.

I scoot into the bench, notice the space in between the tabletop and my stomach, and look across at Wolfgang, who is downing his second carton of milk.

He nods.

I glance back over my shoulder, looking for Rat, but he's nowhere to be found. I guess I'm stuck here for the moment. I take a tiny bite of chicken nugget and chew like crazy.

"You won't believe how little she eats now," Whitney announces to the table. My face burns. I feel like an interesting animal at the zoo at feeding time. See how the elephant uses its trunk to pick up the hay off the ground.

I glance around the table to see people watching me chew. Wolfgang is especially interested in what I'm not eating.

"So . . . you're not going to eat all those potatoes, right?"

"No," I say, watching the interest grow in his eyes. "Do you want them?"

"Sure, but next time order the gravy on the side."

I nod. There's evidently going to be a next time for me to sit at the popular table. If only to give Wolfgang my leftovers. I look down the table toward Briella. She's talking to someone on the other side of her. She leans back, laughing and tossing her hair over her shoulder, and I see it's Rat. What's he doing at this table, too? His regular spot is over by the trash cans with the other science geeks. He's never spent a day on this bench before, but he looks like he's been here forever. My stomach feels funny at the way he's smiling back at Briella. Or maybe it's just the chicken nuggets. That's probably what it is.

"Are you full yet?" Whitney watches me like a hawk. I chew my third bite of chicken nugget and finally take a bite of mashed potatoes.

"Almost," I answer.

"Amazing," Whitney says, then addresses the whole table in a loud I-know-all-about-it voice. "She only eats a few bites and feels like she just ate a Thanksgiving dinner. Right, Ever?"

I look around the table. Everyone seems fascinated. With me.

"Yeah," I say.

Whitney looks down her too-big-for-her-face nose at me. "So how much weight have you lost so far?"

"Seventy-two pounds," I tell her. Whitney Stone is asking me a question in front of all her popular friends, and I'm answering her. That's the amazing part.

"That's like one of you," Wolfgang says to Whitney.

"I wish." She makes a fake frowny face and says, "I weigh way more than that, silly."

She turns to Kristen, who always seems to be not too far away from Whitney's left elbow. "You should look into that surgery."

Kristen is maybe twenty pounds overweight. Maybe. Kristen looks down at the tabletop and bites her lip.

"Now, that really hurt. Comparing poor, average-sized Kristen to you."

"You have to be more than a hundred pounds overweight to qualify for the surgery." I can't believe I'm trying to make Kristen Rogers feel better.

"So when will it stop?" Whitney asks.

"I don't know for sure. Most people stop losing weight after about a year."

"So you're only halfway done? You could lose seventy-five more pounds?" Kristen asks incredulously.

"It slows down. I won't lose as fast as I have been."

"I saw this actress on TV that did that surgery. She lost a lot of weight," Kristen says. "But she's gained it all back."

I don't feel sorry for her anymore.

People start scooting together to make room. Jackson slides onto the bench beside Whitney and, more important, beside me. I freeze with a chicken nugget halfway to my mouth.

"Hey, Ever," Jackson says like it's not even unusual that I'm sitting here. I smile back at him and put the half-eaten nugget back down on my tray. I'm eating lunch with Jackson. I glance down the table, trying to take it all in, and catch Rat looking back. He's not smiling anymore. He gives me a subtle thumbs-up sign. Just for me. I nod ever so slightly. It's happening. I'm at the popular table. I'm sitting beside Jackson, not on top of a broken chair with everyone laughing at me. It's all good.

Right?

"You're just a freak show," Skinny whispers. *"They're just grateful for a little entertainment, Frankenstein."*

I look down at my food, blinking a couple of times to clear my head. Jackson's hand is there, lying on the table right beside my chicken nuggets. The same hand that touched my face. Stroked my hair. So very close. If I just moved my arm a little to the left I would touch him.

"You going to eat that?" Wolfgang asks, jolting me out of my daydream. I shake my head and he pulls my tray across the table to line it up beside his, scooping mashed potatoes up and over to his plate.

"This is going to work out great," he says, between bites of my leftover chicken nuggets.

After school, I sit on my front steps, tying my shoelaces in advance of my run. Roxanne is sitting beside me with her leash in her mouth, trying to wait patiently, but her whole backside is wiggling on the concrete. I look up to see Dad turn in the driveway in his sheriff's car, and I give him a wave.

He joins me and Roxanne on the steps. "How was school?" It's his go-to question.

"Good." That is my go-to answer.

"Have any homework?" Question number two. Like clockwork.

"I already did it. Arrest any bad guys today?" My turn for the routine question.

His answer to this question is never the same, which is always my favorite part of our first conversation of the evening.

"John David Kelly. Shot his son because he wouldn't get off the phone and go feed the cows," he says, pushing Roxanne's enthusiastic welcome away from his face.

"Dead?" I figure he isn't or Dad wouldn't have told me about it. He keeps the serious cases to himself.

"Nope. It was buckshot. Painful, but not lethal."

"Is he going to jail?"

"Probably not. He's ninety-two and his son's not pressing charges. I told him he needs to think about putting his dad in one of those assisted-living places, though. One without shotguns."

"Or phones," I say, and laugh. I stand up and stretch my calves out with a lunge on the step.

"How's the running going?" Dad asks.

"I can make it all the way to the mailbox now without stopping." I grin at him.

"You look wonderful." He stands up and gives me a quick hug. "I'm proud of you, Ever."

"He's proud of you because of the way you LOOK," Skinny whispers in the earbud of my iPod when I push it into my ears. I turn up the music loud — "I Am Changing" from *Dreamgirls* — and wave good-bye. Dad stands on the porch and watches Roxanne and me. We jog slowly off down the sidewalk.

Mrs. Burns waves at me from her flower bed and I see her mouth moving.

I pull out an earbud. "What?"

"Looking good!" she calls out.

I smile back at her, the unfamiliar feeling of pride soaring into my heart and quickening my steps. "Thanks!"

I pass dead Cat Lady's house and keep running, wiping the sweat off my face with the shoulder of my T-shirt. Roxanne's tongue is hanging out of her mouth as she pants happily along beside me. I think about my day and I keep running. Jackson talked to me and said I looked good. I sat at the popular table.

When I reach the mailbox, I'm not out of breath. I start to think about the flyer for musical tryouts. Rat is right, but then he is always right. Drama class is the only thing keeping me from that stage and getting Jackson back. If I want a part in the musical I have to take drama. Drama class means silly acting exercises in front of a whole class full of critics. If I were someone like Gigi, I would love it. But the thought of all those eyes fills me with dread. Skinny would have a field day.

I keep going for five more blocks before I slow down into a walk. I have a 3.95 GPA average in all honors classes, how hard can one stupid drama class be?

That night, when I step off the scale, I add the three more pounds lost on my chart and record the exercise. I wish Rat were here to see it.

"One mile? Please. Like that's something to brag about."

Rat was nowhere to be found after school, so I took the bus home. But it's Rat. He'll be back, right? I'll fix it. Somehow.

	Weight	Pounds Lost	Exercise	Playlist
STARTING WEIGHT: 302 HEIGHT: 5'6"				
Week 17	227	75	Run (1 mile)	"I Am Changing" (*Dreamgirls*)

CHAPTER FOURTEEN

M s. DeWise is the youngest teacher at Huntsville High School. Or at least she looks that way. Maybe it's because she always wears jeans rolled up to show her black Ed Hardy tennis shoes with the red broken heart on them. Or maybe it's her red curly hair that is obviously not "born with it" red, but more like "let's find the reddest red ever to come out of a box" red. Everything about her screams drama, and that's why I've avoided her classes at all cost. There's no telling what she'll ask a student to do, and the almost impossible odds of me being able to blend into the back wall make her, and her teaching, a complete nightmare for me.

Unfortunately, as Rat pointed out last week, I have to take drama in order to try out for the musical. Stupid rule.

Too bad he's still avoiding me, or I'd tell him I'd signed up for the class. I need to tell him I'm sorry and that I miss his weird science experiments and constant monitoring. I need to say I miss him. And I will tell him. Soon.

But I've gone this far. Risked death by stomach rearrangement, trips to the mall with Whitney, and maybe even losing my best friend, to get to this point. Now all that stands between me trying out for the musical and wowing everyone as Cinderella is Ms. DeWise's drama class. So here I am, sitting in the middle of a class full of theater nerds, my palms sweating and my breath coming in short little gasps, trying not to draw any attention to myself. But that is the problem. Drama is all about attention.

"Everybody up," Ms. DeWise calls out as soon as she enters the room, her clown hair bouncing wildly around her head with each step. In the front row, Gigi leaps up and immediately starts doing jumping jacks. Others, obviously in the know, get up and start stretching legs and arms. I stand there awkwardly, waiting for instructions, sure that everyone is watching me.

"Stretch. Up, up, up to the ceiling. Inhale."

I raise my arms, fingers extending, and glance around the room. No one is looking at me. They are all stretching. I suck in a breath and hold it awkwardly.

"Okay, relax!" Ms. DeWise shouts. "Go limp from your waist up. Drop your arms down to the floor. Sweeping. Sweeping."

I bend over and let my arms drop toward my feet. I keep sneaking looks around the room out of the corners of my eyes, trying to make sure I'm doing it right.

"Exhale." Ms. DeWise paces back and forth in front of us. "Couple of deep breaths. Slowly. In. Out. In. Out."

Slowly, everyone straightens with some groans and relaxed

laughter. Okay, it's over. I did it. I try to escape back into my desk.

Not going to happen.

"Everyone down on the floor."

She's kidding, right? I look around, pulling up my once again baggy jeans. Apparently, she isn't. Everyone is pushing away desks and lying down on their backs. I sink down to my knees, roll back onto my butt slowly, and awkwardly extend my legs out in front of me.

So clumsy. You can't even lie down gracefully. Look at Gigi up there. She looks like she's dancing even when she lies down.

I position my backpack behind me and lie back, using it as a pillow. I stare up at the ceiling tiles, noticing a water-stained corner on the one directly above my head.

"Everyone, close your eyes." I shut my eyes halfway, but close them when I see her Ed Hardys marching up the aisle. "I want everyone to relax their bodies and minds. Think the answers to my questions. Concentrate on quieting your spirit. Ready?"

I guess so.

"Who's beside you? Who's in front? Who's in back?"

I have no idea. I know Gigi is in front of the room. I did notice her. I could describe the ceiling tiles, but she doesn't ask about that.

"What process did you go through this morning before you came to school? Did you take a shower? Did you eat breakfast? Go through each step before you came to school."

I ate breakfast. A quarter of a bagel and a spoonful of cream cheese. Then I fought with Briella over her excessive bathroom time. Remembering the way she threw her hairbrush at me doesn't relax me.

"Now think of a sad moment. What is happening to make you feel so sad? Where are you? What do the surroundings look like?"

The memory of my mom in the hospital cafeteria comes out of nowhere and shocks through my body, causing my hands to twitch uncontrollably at my sides. It's like this movie I saw once where these people were on a luxury cruise ship and they were having a fancy dinner party, totally unaware that this huge tidal wave was coming.

In the memory, in the hospital cafeteria, people are eating and talking and trying to be as normal as possible. Even though there are wheelchairs and IV poles and lots of hats covering bald heads. And there is the tidal wave — cancer — coming toward the big sunny windows outside. Every family in this cafeteria will be washed away, including mine, will be turned upside down, torn apart by this huge, random tidal wave, and there is nothing any of us can do to predict when it will hit. We can't stop it, either. So everyone eats their Jell-O cups and drinks their juice through plastic straws and ignores that huge looming wave right outside the window.

I squeeze my eyelids shut tightly. Not relaxing.

Thankfully, Ms. DeWise interrupts the moment with a new shouted command. "Now think of a happy moment. What was going on during that time? On the count of three, shout out one word to describe that happy moment." I can hear Ms. DeWise marching around the room now, confidently yelling out her questions. "One . . . two . . . three."

I think of Jackson and I whisper the word, "Snow."

A male voice next to me shouts, "Party."

"Wonderful!" Ms. DeWise claps her hands. I hear the noise of people stirring around me and open my eyes a peep. Everyone is getting up off the floor. Evidently, I survived the opening exercises. I slide back into my desk and watch Ms. DeWise warily for her next move. She pulls chairs to the front of the room. There are three chairs facing the rows of students.

"Gigi." She motions for her to sit in the first chair. She calls Chance Lehmann up for the second chair, and he saunters up to the stage smiling and waving to the class. Then, horror of horrors, she calls my name.

"Ever." She picks the chair up and moves it up a little closer to the audience. "Take the last chair here."

I shuffle up to the front and sit down in the chair, staring down at my feet and feeling a little like I'm going to throw up.

Ms. DeWise rests her hand on my shoulder. "Everyone give a round of applause to our volunteers!"

I didn't volunteer. Everyone claps politely.

"This semester we'll be using familiar folk and fairy tales for our exercises. Today we're going to work with *Sleeping Beauty*." Ms. DeWise puts her arm around the back of my chair and squats down between Chance and me. "In just a few minutes, when I give the signal, all three of our volunteers are going to transform themselves into Sleeping Beauty."

Chance sweeps pretend hair back from his shoulders dramatically and bats his eyes. The class laughs. I sit there and swallow and swallow.

"In this scene, Sleeping Beauty has been left alone in the woods." Ms. DeWise brushes a red curl back from her forehead and it immediately springs back into place. "She's deserted. Lonely. Dejected."

I glance up at the audience and then back down at my feet.

"How are you going to be the star of the musical when you can't even do this? You're going to blow it and then everyone will think you're totally, completely incompetent," whispers Skinny, *"and you are."*

"When I clap my hands, I want each of you to look like Sleeping Beauty at this moment. Ready?"

We all nod and she slaps her hands together.

I frown and try to look as sad as possible. I throw in a little bit of scared, too. That part isn't very hard.

"No! All wrong!" Ms. DeWise slaps her hands together again, and I almost jump out of my chair. She's addressing all of us, but I feel like she's only talking to me. "You all look like you are *acting* sad, not like you are *really* sad. Actors can't just make up emotions. In life, feelings are the result of something that happened that affected you. Feelings don't just happen without *something* causing the reaction."

My stomach churns.

Ms. DeWise puts her hand on my shoulder again. "That *something* is what you think of when you're onstage — the something that causes you to feel a certain way, when the audience was not there to pressure you to perform. Let's try this again."

Groan.

"So think about a time when you felt left out and rejected. When everyone had turned their backs on you . . ."

When did I *not* feel that way?

"Think about exactly what was happening when you felt that way," Ms. DeWise says, stepping in front of the three chairs and scrutinizing each one of her volunteers.

A day comes to mind with a stage and a chair crashing to the floor. Blood rushes to my cheeks. I feel caught, a deer in headlights. A slow familiar panic takes over my body. There is nowhere to hide. I push the memory away. I don't want to think about that.

"Wait, Ever." I'm startled by Ms. DeWise's voice. "It was there on your face for a minute. You were remembering something, right?"

I nod, reluctantly. Panic starts to rise into my throat. I can't say it out loud. Please don't ask me to.

"And I saw it. In your eyes. In the way you held your body. Everything about you looked exactly like Sleeping Beauty would have looked when she was left behind in the woods. Dejected. Alone. Isolated." Ms. DeWise bursts into applause, and the audience joins in enthusiastically. "Bravo! Well done, Ever!"

Acting like Sleeping Beauty means not thinking about Sleeping Beauty? I'm confused, but I have to admit a little intrigued. I also feel pretty good about the applause.

"You can go back to your seats," Ms. DeWise says. She brings up a few more volunteers and I find myself watching the action carefully. Each time the group portrays a different fairy-tale character and another strong emotion. Some do it better than others. I know the difference when I see it, but I'm still not sure how it happens.

"Good work today." Ms. DeWise finally releases the last set of three students back to their desks. "Now for your homework."

There are loud groans throughout the room.

"Everyone, draw a slip of paper on your way out the door today. On the slip of paper will be an animal." I don't like the way this is going. I was hoping to play the part of a princess, not a monkey. "I want you to study it and be very specific in your observation of the animal. What is the animal's posture? How does he move? When does he move? *Why* does he move? Can you imagine what he might be thinking?"

"Do you expect us to go to the zoo tonight?" Chance asks and gets a few laughs.

"You can find anything on the Internet," Ms. DeWise says. "Find as many different clips of this animal in action as you can. After you watch awhile, begin physically imitating his movements. Be as specific as possible."

"Are you sure about that?" Chance asks. "I've been told plenty of times to stop monkeying around."

Oh, brother. Why does Chance always have to be a clown?

Ms. DeWise isn't fazed. "If it's a gorilla you are studying, and the gorilla places its hand somewhere on its body in such a way that you might not place your hand on your body, especially in public, then you must overcome your inhibitions."

There is some more nervous laughter as students head toward the door.

Ms. DeWise gives one last set of directions while handing out the slips of paper to the students leaving the room. "Keep the physical and psychological aspects of the animal. Just transform them to the human counterpart in yourself. Study the animal for as long and as often as you can. Then come back to the workshop next Monday prepared to share your interpretation."

I draw a slip of paper out of her hand as I leave the room, then instantly stuff it down into my pocket. Later, with no one around to see, I pull it out and open it. Elephant. My heart sinks. I couldn't have picked giraffe, or butterfly, or swan?

"The fat girl gets to pretend to be an elephant. I think they'll call it typecasting."

I'm not giving up. Jackson will see me play the role of Cinderella, and I will win him back. Even if I have to be an elephant to do it.

That night, I look at every elephant video I can find on the Internet. Only elephants in the wild, though, because I want to see what they look like when they're at home — not in a cage. I try to focus on the animal's eyes. Does it seem intelligent? Tame? Wild? Dangerous? I try to imagine thinking like an elephant. I wonder what I'm thinking when the elephant in one video moves from the spot where she had been standing for quite some time to a tree fifty feet away to pick a few leaves to eat. Why did she move now, and not five minutes ago?

I find this one video where a huge bull elephant crashes out of the brush to charge a camera crew in the back of a truck. The elephant isn't clumsy. He doesn't cower. He bursts through the trees large and in charge, ears flapping wildly. He's perfectly comfortable in his size and knows exactly how to use it.

I watch it again.

I can't imagine any other animal intimidating him. He moves with a speed terrifying to everyone in the back of that truck watching. Nothing stands in his way.

I watch it again.

Amazing. He relishes every bit of his size. This is the kind of elephant I want to be. I stand up in front of the computer.

I watch the video again, but this time I move around the room as I watch it. Now, the elephant has legs and arms.

I don't cower or waddle. I walk like a huge elephant.

And I like it.

	Weight	Pounds Lost	Exercise	Playlist
STARTING WEIGHT: 302 HEIGHT: 5'6"				
Week 20	220	82	Run (1 mile)	"I Whistle a Happy Tune" (*The King and I*)

"So when the actor becomes aware of being observed by others out there" — Ms. DeWise waves to the seats out in the auditorium — "the tension finds its way into the actor's life on the stage. The key word here is 'aware.'"

I'm back in drama class and today we're meeting in the auditorium for the first time. All I can think about is what's going to happen when I take the stage pretending to be an elephant. I'm definitely aware.

"When the actor first becomes *aware* of being observed by an audience, it causes the actor to suffer that state of self-consciousness that we sometimes call stage fright," Ms. DeWise continues her lecture from center stage, her arms sweeping widely to emphasize the importance of her words to everyone listening.

I'm always aware of being observed. Always self-conscious. I'm evidently living my life with stage fright.

"So the trick here is not allowing oneself to become aware of the audience."

Duh. The idea of that seems completely impossible to me, but oh so attractive.

"Let me show you a little demonstration," Ms. DeWise continues. "Gigi, if you'll come up to the stage."

Gigi flits up the stage steps and joins Ms. DeWise. This week, her hair is all blue with just a streak of pink on the left side and she's wearing a red-striped T-shirt with skinny blue jeans. Sparkling chandelier earrings wobble wildly from side to side as she waves energetically to the class. A pretty tame outfit for Gigi.

"I've asked Gigi to help me with this exercise." Ms. DeWise steps over to stage left and leaves Gigi standing alone in the middle of the stage. I feel a twinge of jealousy at how effortlessly she faces the room full of people watching her.

"Onstage we have three walls," says Ms. DeWise. "The one in back and on each side."

Gigi gestures in each direction as Ms. DeWise talks, like she's a flight attendant showing the exits.

"The fourth wall, that very important wall between the actors and the audience, is invisible. If the actors don't acknowledge the audience behind that fourth wall, then everyone watching the action onstage is able to believe they are peering into the secret lives of the people onstage as if they were in their own kitchens or bedrooms."

Gigi pretends to sit down at a table and eat imaginary food.

"So here you have the actor." Ms. DeWise points to Gigi, who continues to pantomime eating as though we aren't watching her. "Then you have the invisible fourth wall." Ms. DeWise makes a sweeping motion signaling the front of the stage with one hand. Finally, she points to all of us watching. "And the audience."

Gigi pretends to pick up a phone off an imaginary table and dials, while we all watch.

Ms. DeWise continues, "When we use a fourth wall in a play, the actors don't acknowledge there is anyone watching them and the audience is able to suspend disbelief and pretend the actors are actually living out their real lives onstage."

"Hello?" Gigi says into her pretend phone. "Is Cinderella there?"

The audience laughs, but Gigi keeps talking, looking blankly out at the audience as if she is staring absently at a painting on the wall. "I just got my invitation to the ball yesterday. Are you going?" She waits as though she's listening to the response from the other end of the phone conversation, then continues, "I don't have anything to —"

"Okay, freeze," Ms. DeWise commands, and Gigi stops midsentence. "Now as you saw, Gigi was looking directly at the audience, but she made believe the audience didn't exist. That's what the fourth wall is all about."

A fourth wall in life. How great would that be? I'd never have to worry what people thought about me again. The wall would keep it all out.

"Now, Gigi's going to show you how to break this fourth wall," Ms. DeWise says, and then turns back to the frozen Gigi. "Action!"

"Have you heard from your fairy godmother lately?" Gigi continues her fake conversation with Cinderella on the phone, still looking out into the audience as she talks. Suddenly, she focuses in directly on Chance Lehmann in the front row, lowers the imaginary phone from her ear, and says, "Excuse me, you there in the audience with the blue shirt, do you mind not yawning? Have a mocha or something and stay awake, will you?"

The audience laughs in appreciation and, just like that, the illusion of a real phone conversation is shattered along with the separation between the audience and the actor.

"Freeze," Ms. DeWise commands, and instantly Gigi is motionless and quiet on the stage. "Our actor just did a terrific job of demonstrating what breaking the fourth wall looks like, and all of you were able to see the moment when our actor became aware of the audience."

Kristen is sitting two rows in front of me. I see her curly head bob up and down in agreement.

"Today, we're going to work on not letting that happen. We want to make our audiences believe the story that's taking place onstage. One way to accomplish this is for an actor to concentrate on something specific while delivering the lines. If you're able to do that, it's impossible to concentrate on the audience," Ms. DeWise says. "Let's give Gigi a round of applause."

Everyone claps politely as Gigi takes her seat.

"Now it's your turn." Ms. DeWise moves back to center stage. "For today's exercise, I will put each of you into a small group. Your homework for this week, and the animal you selected, will be the thing for you to concentrate on. However, I don't want you to let the others know what your chosen object of attention is. As you will see, the result of this simple, common exercise can be startling."

"People will be laughing at you. Everywhere. Looking at you. And you want to make it worse by trying to look more like an elephant?"

Ms. DeWise calls people to the stage. I'm relieved to not be in the first group, but it just delays the inevitable. A bead of sweat rolls down my back.

"Today our framework will be the familiar fairy tale *Cinderella*," she says in her projecting voice. "But all of you will be applying your homework to your characters. I want you to focus completely on the movements, mannerisms, and look of your chosen animal as you deliver your lines."

A dark-haired girl named Shelly delivers her lines as the fairy godmother with a short, chirpy voice and quick steps around center stage. I'm guessing her animal is a bird of some kind. Cinderella, a short boy with unlaced tennis shoes that look like they might fall off at any minute, talks with a bit of a whine to his voice. At one point he jumps onto the couch and stretches his arms out over his head, extending each finger carefully like claws. A cat. I can see it now.

The scene is over and everyone applauds. I realize I've been so busy watching the action on the stage I've forgotten to be nervous. It all comes back the minute Ms. DeWise calls my name. She also calls up Kristen, Gigi, and Natalie Vance, a tall girl I know from my English class. We stand awkwardly at the side of the stage, as Ms. DeWise briefs us on the scene. The two stepsisters (Kristen and Natalie) are talking with Cinderella (Gigi) when the stepmother (me) enters the scene to tell everyone about the upcoming ball. The stepsisters are thrilled, but Cinderella is crushed to discover she won't be able to go.

Pretty simple. Of course I know the story. I'm living it. It's just that I usually envision myself as Cinderella, not the stepmother. But it's acting, right? I move offstage to wait for my big entrance.

"I don't want to do this." Kristen is actually talking to me. I glance over at her. She doesn't look so good, rubbing her hands together and biting her lip anxiously.

"What's wrong?"

"I didn't even want to take this stupid class. My mom thought it would help me with cheerleading tryouts," she whispers loudly. "I think I'm going to throw up."

"No, you're not." I gently push her out from behind the curtain. "You're on."

I cross my arms in front of me tight against my body, holding in the rising nerves and trying to pull myself together. Don't think about the audience. Put up that fourth wall.

"You're going to act like an elephant in front of everyone? What a surprise. Everyone's been comparing you to one for years. And the Academy Award goes to . . . the elephant who looks just like an elephant."

Gigi is a Cinderella monkey, I think. It's not a good combination, although her wild jumping and shrieking is getting plenty of laughs from the audience. I think one stepsister is some kind of dog, but I have no clue what Kristen is supposed to be. Maybe a mouse? She's twitching her nose a lot. That might just be her nerves.

It's time for my entrance. Elephant. Powerful. Awe-inspiring. Not afraid of using my size. I imagine my huge ears flapping in anger, and I stomp out onto the stage to deliver my first line.

The scene is over before I know it and the clapping is loud and appreciative. I was concentrating so hard on being an elephant, I completely lost track of everything else. Evidently that was the point. We all take a bow at the front of the stage. Kristen gives me a big smile. I glance behind me, just to make sure, but it's true. She's smiling at me. I give her a thumbs-up.

"Very good," Ms. DeWise calls out. She's smiling widely and clapping along with the audience. I bow once more, feeling positively giddy with the attention.

"That was great, Ever," Gigi says as we take our seats back in the auditorium. She sits beside me. Like we're friends.

"Thanks," I say. "You were good, too."

"I never knew you had a drama streak. You're usually so quiet and . . ."

"Fat?" Skinny asks.

"And?" I ask.

"I don't know." Gigi pauses, searching for the right word. She finally comes up with one. "Angry."

It isn't what I was expecting.

"Angry at who?"

"I'm not sure. School? Drama club?" Her voice gets smaller and more hesitant. Her brow wrinkles into deep lines. "Me?"

Gigi thought I was angry with her? Why? I don't even know her. "Of course I'm not angry at you," I say.

I don't have time to talk to her anymore because Ms. DeWise calls out for quiet so the next group of actors can begin their scene. I watch it, but I keep thinking about what Gigi said.

"She's never liked you. You know that," Skinny hisses.

Do I know that? Thinking back, I can't remember a time I've ever actually had a real conversation with Gigi.

Was that my choice or hers?

THE BALL

CHAPTER SIXTEEN

On the first Saturday in October, Whitney pushes me out of the way and descends on the mahogany desk at the Headhunters Salon and Day Spa in the Galleria. I can't believe I let her drive me all the way to Houston for a hair appointment, but I have to admit I've been pleasantly surprised by her previous makeover experiments on me. Briella is at her dad's this weekend, but Whitney says we can't wait for her to go with us. It's too hard to get an appointment with Lawrence, her special stylist, and evidently Whitney had to pull a lot of strings for him to even consider taking on a new client.

"We would like to speak to Lawrence," she says to the receptionist, with a determined glint in her eye.

"Do you have an appointment?" The woman at the desk is a gorgeous platinum blonde without a trace of a smile on her carefully painted bow lips. Her perfectly manicured fuchsia fingernail remains pointed at the appointment book to hold her place.

"He's expecting us." Whitney gives the receptionist a frosty response. "Just tell him Whitney is here."

"I'll see if he's available." The blonde sounds doubtful as she stands and glides off silently down a beige-carpeted hall.

"Come on." Whitney walks over to the pink swivel chairs underneath a picture of purple irises. She settles in with two of the Godiva chocolates from the etched-glass dish on the coffee table.

"Looks like Lawrence is doing all right." Whitney glances around the elegant pink- and beige-drenched room. "This is a long way from the Glory to God Laundry Mat and Beauty Parlor." Whitney reaches for another treat.

I wait for a further explanation, but Whitney nibbles quietly on a third piece of candy with only an occasional sigh of satisfaction. My eyebrows go up in surprise. I've never seen her eat more than one bite of anything, but now she's downed three pieces of chocolate in five minutes.

"Chocolate," she breathes. "It's my one fatal flaw. I'd offer you one, but, you know . . ." She pauses for dramatic effect. "Dumping syndrome."

Since Whitney took me on as her project, she also felt the need to become an Internet expert on gastric bypass surgery. "Dumping," as she now knows, is when food passes too quickly into the small intestine. It typically happens when a gastric bypass patient eats a sugary food. I "dumped" once in July when I tried to eat ice cream. Once was enough. My heart beat rapidly and forcefully while my body tried to adjust. I broke into a cold sweat and had to lie down for about thirty minutes. It was a scary feeling and it ought to make me want to stay far away from anything sweet, but I still jealously eye the chocolate in Whitney's hand. Old habits are so hard to break even when they make you sick.

"Who do you want to ask you to the Fall Ball?" Whitney's eyes narrow with the importance of the question, as she waves around the half-eaten piece of chocolate for emphasis.

It's a trick question. She knows no one is going to ask YOU to a dance," Skinny whispers.

"I haven't thought about it," I say. *Jackson,* I think.

"Oh, I know you have," Whitney says, with a sly smile. She pops the last bite of temptation into her mouth and then talks around the chewing. "I saw the way you looked at Jackson Barnett the other day."

"He's an old friend," I say. I need to change the subject. "What about you?"

"I'm thinking I'll go with Matt Leland." Matt is the tall, redheaded star basketball player who sends Whitney endless text messages.

"He's cute," I say. It's an understatement and we both know it. He's gorgeous.

"We should double-date." Whitney claps her hands together in delight at this idea.

"He already asked you? I didn't know you already had a date." I'm obviously confused. Of course Whitney Stone would have a date to the dance. Stupid me.

She laughs. "I don't yet, silly. It's still three weeks away."

"But you will," I say, slowly.

"Of course." She says it like I'm brainless. "And you will, too. You'll see."

"What about Briella?" I ask. Whitney and Briella are still best friends, right?

"I imagine she'll go with Wolf."

"No, I meant don't you want to double-date with her?"

"She can come with us if she wants. . . ." Whitney's voice trails off dubiously.

Am I replacing Briella as Whitney's new BFF? When Whitney's friend-spotlight shines on you, it's a whole lot of work.

"Lawrence will see you now." Startled at the sudden interruption, I look up to see the blonde is back, waiting expressionlessly by the opening to a long hallway.

Suddenly I have no desire to see the mysterious Lawrence McIntire, but I'm committed now. All I can do is self-consciously tug down my comfortable, now oversized, brown sweater, pull up my baggy jeans, and follow Joy, the receptionist, down the long corridor.

The cream-colored carpet is so thick my tennis shoes sink into it with each step.

"You don't belong in a place like this," Skinny says.

In the room off to the right, a red-haired manicurist adds the final touches to a white poodle's toenails as the tiny woman holding him looks on in delight.

"I think you were right, Monique. Misty Rose is just the right color for both of us," I hear the woman exclaim as we continue down the hall.

Farther down the hall on the left, a white lab-coated attendant in pink high-heeled pumps applies cucumber slices to a reclining woman in a giant pink smock. Her face is covered completely with some kind of green mud.

"The process has begun," announces Lab Coat. The green goo cracks slightly in what I assume is a smile. "Just wait. You're going to be simply amazed at the outcome."

Lab Coat looks up at us as we pass and frowns.

"What is someone like you doing here?"

I'm starting to panic. Idon'twanttodothis. Idon'twanttodothis. It's all I can do to keep from turning and running back down the hall and out the front doors.

We stop at the end of the hallway in front of two closed, elaborately carved wooden doors. Joy grasps the gold brass handles and looks back over her left shoulder to see if we are following. Unfortunately, we are. After throwing back the doors with a dramatic flourish, Joy waves us into the room.

A clutter of scissors, brushes, sprays, and gels are scattered across a single table on the wall opposite the doors. A large barber's chair is placed right in the center of the room. On the wall beside the doorway is the only decoration — a six-foot stuffed shark mounted with a mouth wide open and full of teeth, ready to gobble up anything that swims, or walks, by. There are no mirrors. I feel my left eye begin to twitch.

"Please make yourselves comfortable. I'll tell Lawrence you're ready for him." Joy glides out, leaving us standing in the middle of the room alone.

But only for a few minutes.

"Whitney, my dear! How wonderful you look." Lawrence sweeps into the room with a whirl of a gray smock, gathering Whitney into his arms for a quick hug. As he pulls away, he fingers a strand of her hair. "I think you're due for highlights."

"Not today. I brought you a present." Whitney nods toward me, and Lawrence turns to focus all of his attention on me. I stay by the door, hoping for a quick escape.

Lawrence is over six feet tall, with a biker's build. The sleeves of his gray smock are cut away at the shoulders, revealing bulging arm muscles circled with a tattoo of barbed wire. His thick black hair is well past his shoulders and tied back into a ponytail with a brown leather strip. Bright blue eyes contrast sharply with at least a day's growth of stubble.

"Turn around please. . . ." His voice is strangely soft, almost a whisper. He continues his scrutiny while I comply. "Not so fast. Slow down."

Suddenly he stalks across the room and grabs a handful of my hair. He feels the texture and weight with one hand, his face deep in thought. To my astonishment, his eyes suddenly fill with tears.

"Look up toward the light." Lawrence's voice breaks. Is he actually going to cry?

I obey. I see him out of the corner of my eye staring at my face, blinking away the emotion.

"You were right to bring her to me, Whitney," he says, finally, with a sigh. "She is the perfect raw material."

"Have I ever let you down?" Whitney asks. She waves to me, then leaves the room and shuts the door behind her.

"Have a seat." Lawrence motions toward the beauty-shop chair in the middle of the room, and I sit down carefully. He immediately drops down on one knee in front of me, one hand on either side of the chair. I lean back away from him as far as possible.

"Those green eyes are so expressive," he says, after a moment of silent staring. I blink back at him uncomfortably and wish I were anywhere else but here. He continues, "I can tell you are bigger inside than people know."

"Now you're big on the outside and the inside," Skinny whispers.

"Being called big isn't exactly a compliment," I say.

He surprises me with a deep laugh that seems to come out of nowhere. "Trust me, honey. It's so much better than being small on the inside." He winks at me. "I spent a lot of time with small-minded people when I was growing up. Being a hairstylist isn't always considered the most manly of jobs in this neck of the woods. But a hairstylist is all I ever wanted to be. People looked right through me. Never saw me."

I glance down at the thick muscles of his biceps. "I can't imagine anyone would ever look past you," I say.

"You learn to trust your insides and it gets better," he says, standing up quickly and twirling my chair around. "Much better."

"How do you know," I ask, "that people have something big on the inside?"

"It's a gift." Lawrence snaps the cape behind my neck and pats me once on the shoulder. "I recognize people hiding inside themselves. I see it and I help others see it, too."

I take a deep breath.

"Then let's do it," I say quietly, and I'm rewarded with another huge laugh from Lawrence.

It's almost an hour later when Lawrence spins the chair back around to face him. I still haven't seen a mirror and have no idea what the results are of all the cutting and spraying and clipping and blow-drying. He doesn't speak. He only stares down at me in silence, his expression narrowed, and I can't tell if it is bad or good. Finally, he nods solemnly.

"It's done," he says.

I don't know what I'm supposed to say, so I don't say anything.

Suddenly he starts yelling over his shoulder and I almost jump out of the chair. "Come in here!" He stalks over to the wooden doors and throws them open with a flourish, calling out down the hallway. "Whitney!"

I see her walking down the hall toward us with two chocolates in her hand, still chewing. She stops just inside the door and stares at me.

Her mouth falls open. "Wow," she says.

"I know, right?" he says.

"You've outdone yourself," she says to Lawrence, then to me, "Have you seen yourself?"

I shake my head.

"Get the mirror," Lawrence shouts out, and Joy comes running down the hall with a tiny handheld mirror.

I'm afraid to look, but they both stand waiting for my reaction. Hesitantly, I peer at the reflection. I have to admit it, I like what I see. I look different and, after everything I've been through, different feels good. A faint, wistful smile slowly lights the face of the girl in the reflection. Long-buried hope starts to stir. Terrified, I push it back down.

I quickly hand the mirror back to Lawrence. If I don't stare too long, I can almost ignore the something sad that shifts darkly just behind those green eyes.

"You're still fat and ugly. Ugly. Ugly," Skinny's voice echoes in my ear.

CHAPTER SEVENTEEN

*L*ove the new haircut." Chance Lehmann runs to catch up with me after algebra. "The layers and bangs make those green eyes of yours sparkle."

"It was Whitney's idea." I smile at him. "We drove all the way down to Houston this weekend to meet with a stylist she knows at the Galleria."

"I knew it wasn't anyone in this town. Wow. Just wow." He picks up a handful of my brown hair in one hand. "I wish my hair was this thick and straight. Gorgeous."

I laugh. "And this is the part you're going to like the most." I hold out my hands, palms down.

"Jammin' Jelly!" He grabs my hands in his, leaning down to take a closer look at the newly polished nails. "My favorite!"

I spread my fingers wide and fan my face. "Thanks." I grin at him.

"So what did Rat say about all this?" Chance asks.

"About all what?" I say, all innocent sounding. I open my locker and stick my head inside, hiding my face. "You know, Rat's never been one to focus much on girly stuff."

"*Rat isn't saying anything at all these days. Not to you, anyway.*"

Chance frowns and opens the door of his locker next door. He rummages around in his locker and finally pulls out a worn baseball glove. "So, you and Whitney are all BFFs now?"

"I wouldn't say that, but she's been really supportive."

"Right," Chance says, his eyes narrowing. He slams his locker shut with a clang that makes me jump. "I'd watch that if I were you."

"What do you mean?" But I'm asking it to his back as he disappears into the after-school crowd.

I feel a hand on my shoulder and turn to see Jackson standing by my open locker.

"Hey," I say, my heart instantly responding with rapid beats. "What's up?"

"Nice new haircut," he says, and I blush. God, I'd missed looking into those blue-green eyes. "It looks almost like how you used to wear it. You know. Back when we were . . . friends."

"You remember that?"

"Of course," he says. He reaches out to pick up a strand of my hair from my shoulder. "Hanging out back then was amazing, right?"

"Yeah," I say. "It was." An excited hum starts up in my ears. Something's happening. Something big.

"So, anyway, I was wondering if you'd like to go to the dance?" Jackson asks, slowly twisting the strand of hair around his finger. He's standing in front of me and his lips are moving, but I must be misunderstanding what he's saying. He couldn't possibly be asking me out.

"The Fall Ball?" Stupid. Of course he is talking about the Fall Ball. It isn't like we have millions of different dances. There is only one dance a semester and this is it — the biggie — and it is only a few weeks away.

"Whitney said we could go with her and her date. I mean . . . if you want to." He's standing so close I can see his impossibly long eyelashes batting up and down over those amazing sea-colored eyes. I feel an uncomfortable tug at my heart.

"Ummm . . ." I try to process the information. He's really saying this, right? It's not another one of my daydreams. I want to pinch him or me, but I don't think that's the right response. I'm supposed to say something. Our eyes lock, and he breaks into a slow smile.

"Come on. It'll be fun."

"Yes," I say finally, because I realize he's waiting in front of me for an actual answer. Like there would ever be a doubt I'd want to go with him. "That sounds great."

"Good." He runs a hand through his dark hair, and his eyes meet mine for a long moment. I can hardly breathe. "So I'll talk to you later, then?"

"Sure," I mumble in a daze, and watch as he walks off down the hall. As the realization of what just happened starts to set in, I can hardly keep from jumping up and down and squealing like those girls I can't stand. The thin, pretty ones who always gather outside the boy's gym. Jackson. Asked. Me. Out.

Take that, Skinny.

She doesn't respond. She misses a lot of these opportunities lately. The long silences between us are unexpected and strange.

"You want a ride home?" I'm startled by the sudden appearance of Rat at my right elbow.

"Are you actually talking to me?" I smile uneasily and try to make it a joke, but I'm not rewarded with one of the famous Rat smiles in return. We've shared everything since we were five, but never an awkward pause like this one.

He finally breaks the silence. "I'm going by the community center, and I know the kids would like to see you."

"Okay. That'd be good. Let me get my books." I fumble around in my locker, still trying to process what just happened with Jackson. Now I also have Rat to consider. We haven't talked in the last few weeks, and now's my chance to say all the things I've needed to say to make it right. The problem is, the only thing I want to tell him right now is how Jackson just asked me to the ball. Of course, I want to tell Rat first. He knows exactly what it means to me. Everything. I just don't think he wants to hear it anymore.

There's so much I want to say to him, but I can't bring myself to speak. Not yet. He starts the car, and we drive out of the school parking lot, the silence stretching out again. I'm desperate to say something, anything, but the words don't come, and the seconds run by.

Finally I can't stand it anymore. I squeeze my eyes shut and blurt it out. "I'm really sorry for what I said to you. I didn't mean it."

Rat is quiet. I open my eyes and look at his profile. His glasses. The tiny bump on his nose. The place where the dimples would be if he were smiling. But he's not.

"I was just scared to try out for the musical. I mean, it's a big step for me, you know?"

He nods but doesn't take his eyes off the road. "I know," he says.

"Of course you know," I say. "You always know everything."

"Not everything," he says, and the silence stretches out again. I look out the passenger-side window and watch a balding old man walk his basset hound down the street. They turn right at the corner and we go straight. My face is a ghostly half reflection in the window, and I try to think of something more to say. I turn back to Rat and try again.

"I'm doing well in theater class. You'd be shocked to see me up on that stage." I realize I'm talking really fast now, but I just want it to be normal between us again. Like it's always been. "And you should see my playlist. I'm keeping up with it every week."

"Good for you," he says, and it's not sarcastic, but he still seems distant. He breaks for a red light, but keeps his eyes forward on the road. I know this face better than I know my own.

My eyes search the familiar features for some sign. His eyes, his nose, and then . . . his lips.

"I shouldn't have taken it out on you, Rat." I reach out and touch his arm lightly. He glances over at me. "I miss you."

The light changes, and Rat pushes on the gas pedal. "I miss you, too," he says so quietly I barely hear it, but it's enough to make the heaviness lift off my shoulders.

"We're okay?" I ask, as we pull into the community center parking lot. I still need to tell him about Jackson and the dance, but it just doesn't seem like the right time. He'll be happy for me, though. I know he will. So why don't I want to tell him?

"Of course," Rat says.

When we enter the center, Rat goes off in his usual direction, and I head back to the play area.

Mario glances up from a pile of blocks when I enter the room. He gives me a look, and I feel instantly guilty.

"I haven't seen you in a long time," he says. "Rat's been here. But not you."

I kneel down beside him and pick up one of the blocks. "I know," I say, stacking one blue block on top of the two red ones. We take turns for a little while, stacking and rearranging colors in silence.

"Were you sick?" he asks finally, his eyes still on the pile of blocks in front of us.

"Not exactly. I had surgery."

"What's that?"

I think about how to explain it. "They fix your stomach."

He squints over at me. Then he closes one eye and squints at me again. "Are your eyes bigger?"

"No. I think my face is smaller."

"You know, I'm in first grade now. We go all day, and we don't even take a nap." He pushes at the bottom block on the stack, and they topple over with a crash. For some reason, it makes us both smile. "I might be gone a lot, too, you know," he says.

"First grade is very important," I say. "I can understand how that would keep you very busy."

He nods, very seriously. "I'm learning how to read."

"How's it going?"

"It's harder than it looks."

I laugh.

"Do you want a cookie?" he asks.

"Yes," I say, and I do. The chocolate chip cookies on the tiny table beside us look amazing. "But I can't eat cookies anymore."

"You used to like cookies." He looks at me suspiciously.

"I still like them."

"Did the surgery make you not like cookies?"

"When I eat cookies, I don't feel good. It makes me feel sick."

He looks shocked. "That sucks," he says, and I don't try to tell him not to say that, because it really does. Reaching across the scattered blocks, he pats my hand like I'm an old lady who needs comforting.

"Where are the girls?" I ask, trying to get him off the cookie subject.

"They're outside playing princess and they're all mad because they don't have a prince."

"Not in the prince kind of mood today?"

Mario shakes his head. "What about you? Do you have a prince?"

I remember Jackson and the invitation to the dance. The dizzy, bubbly feeling returns. "Yeah, I kind of do."

"Did he ask you to the ball?" Mario sits back on the carpet, the blocks and cookies forgotten for now.

"Yes," I say with a smile. "He did."

"And you said?" Mario asks, after a minute.

"Are you kidding me? He's the prince. Of course I said yes."

"What's his name?"

"Prince Jackson," I say.

Mario stands up, stretching his tiny body to attention. "Now announcing Princess Ever and Prince Jackson," he says in his loudest voice.

I stand up, too, and curtsey in my best princess manner, my head low and my knees bent deep. When I raise my head, I'm rewarded with a giggle from Mario.

A noise behind us breaks the moment, and I turn. It's happened again. Just like the last time I was here. Rat stands inside the door, staring at me. I meet his gaze. It's like walking into a concrete wall. All the laughter is sucked out of me. I don't know how long he's been standing there but, by the look on his face, I know he's heard about the dance and Jackson. My mind is tangled, my tongue tied.

"Jackson asked me to go to the dance," I tell Rat.

"I heard," Rat says. His face is quite still.

"I was going to tell you. I just didn't have the chance yet."

"I thought we were going to the dance together. You and me."

"But you never asked me."

"Did I have to?"

I look at him, trying to figure out if he's serious. He is. "You don't even like to dance," I say. "Do you even know how?"

"No," he says, so quietly I can hardly hear him.

"It's Jackson, Rat," I say carefully, "and he asked *me*." I don't say the rest: "And I've been hoping for this, waiting for this, for years." I don't need to say it.

"Then I guess I'm happy for you," Rat says. "Congratulations."

Mario leans in against my body and slides his hand in mine. I glance down at his upturned face. I know what he's thinking by his troubled look. Rat doesn't seem happy.

"I'm leaving now, if you want a ride home." Rat's voice is calm as he turns to go.

That night, I dream I lose my computer. I leave it at Jilly's in a booth with all the popular kids and when I go back to get it, it's gone. The night before that I dreamed I lost my iPod. The night before that: my locker. I even lose my way going to biology class and only find the room on the day of the final exam. I spend most of the night wandering around looking for what I've lost.

I wake up tired, like I've actually been walking all over town for the last eight hours instead of sleeping in my bed. The worst part about these dreams is that crazy searching feeling I have in my stomach when I wake up. A feeling that I just HAVE to find whatever it is that's gone.

Even in the shower, fully awake, I keep trying to figure out what exactly I've lost and where it could be. The dream tickles at my mind like that mosquito bite I get in the summer that's right in the middle of my back and no matter how hard I try, I just can't quite touch it. It's so perfectly out of reach that I can't stop thinking about it.

It must be about the weight loss. After all, I've lost enough pounds now to equal one small person. Maybe that's what my subconscious is looking for — that whole person that's missing.

	Weight	Pounds Lost	Exercise	Playlist
STARTING WEIGHT: 302 HEIGHT: 5'6"				
Week 26	203	99	Run (1.5 miles)	"I Could Have Danced All Night" (*My Fair Lady*)

"Turn around," Whitney commands. She stands with her hands on her hips, her eyes narrowed in concentration.

I do as she says, trying not to trip over the long blue dress that spills onto the carpet in a pool around my feet. Strappy, sparkling sandals are lying on the floor by the closet. When I step into them, the dress length will be just right for dancing.

My hair is pulled back from my face and upswept with a ton of bobby pins. Whitney has backcombed the top of it into a poufy bump, and now she leans in to push a sparkly clip into the mass of brown curls. I watch her in the mirror, astonished at the reflection.

Whitney wears a short white wisp of a dress with a deep plunge of a neckline that features her Victoria's Secret–enhanced cleavage. Her perfectly spray-tanned legs are long and lean in four-inch silver Jessica Simpson platform pumps. Fortunately, she was more conservative when she carefully selected my dress.

I never could have dreamed I'd have a mean-girl godmother for the ball. Or that I'd be going to the Fall Ball with Jackson. I could say it a million times and never believe it. Just the thought makes my stomach do a flip. But wait. There's more. I'm double-dating with Whitney Stone and we're all going to the ball in a limo that Whitney's dad paid for. The girl in the mirror smiles back at me, her dark green eyes sparkling with excitement.

Whitney's mom knocks on the door and then pushes her head inside.

"Honey, the boys have been waiting for a while now. Are you ready?"

I slip on the shoes. They aren't glass, but it's just as much a fairy tale. I take one final look in the mirror and my mouth goes dry. The deep blue of the dress sets off my dark hair, making it look darker and shinier. I can see the shape of my waist. I'm not a blob of blubber anymore.

"You're still the fattest girl in the room," Skinny whispers, ever so softly.

We descend each step carefully. I feel a little wobbly, but I'm not sure if it's the new shoes or just my nerves. Whitney's dad stands below, snapping pictures. Jackson is there waiting, corsage in hand. He's wearing a dark blue pinstriped suit with a crisp white shirt and a red striped tie. He looks older and even more gorgeous, if that's possible. The sight of him makes me more nervous than ever.

"Wow." Jackson's mouth falls open in shock when he sees me for the first time. The look on his face is just as I've imagined it. Only now it's real. "You look amazing," he says.

My hand is shaking as he slides the small spray of tiny white roses onto my wrist.

"You're happy, right?" he asks, looking up from my hand to my face. His forehead is creased with concern.

I nod, still not able to speak.

"Pictures!" Whitney crows. "Dad, get a shot of Ever by herself. I need one for my portfolio."

I think she's kidding, but she's not. I feel exposed. The camera is my nemesis. Right up there with mirrors. I smile uncomfortably and try to blend back into the background. After about a hundred shots, we finally shut the limo door and head to the dance. Jackson slides in next to me, puts his arm around my bare shoulders, and pulls me in closer.

"You don't need to sit so far away," he laughs.

It feels strange to be near someone, touching them, and not have them revolted by me. It's even weirder that Skinny has been strangely quiet. She never would have missed such a perfect opportunity in the past, but lately there's been missed moments where her voice is oddly absent. Maybe she's leaving for good, but there's still an uncomfortable beat of silence where her voice should be. The new-and-Whitney-improved me hopes even the nervous pause will go away with time.

Whitney is kissing Matt, her arms wrapped around his neck. She's almost sitting in his lap. Awkward. I glance away, but I'm not sure where I'm supposed to look. Rat thinks Matt is a jerk because he cheated on his chemistry labs. Rat. Stop thinking about Rat. He hasn't talked to me since we went to the community center, so it's obvious he's stopped thinking about me. I've seen him and he nods, but he just keeps going. I hear he's working on the Science Olympiad competition. Very busy. Too busy, evidently, for me.

"Can you believe how great she looks?" Whitney says to Jackson and Matt, when she finally surfaces for air. Now the focus is all on me. "The dress is Ralph Lauren. I found it at Nordstrom. It had to be altered, of course, but I still think it looks fab on her."

"Yeah, pretty unbelievable," Matt says. He studies me like I'm some kind of alien. "I remember just last year you were in my math class, and you were *huge*."

"Thanks, I think," I say, and Jackson pats my leg like he totally understands.

The dance is at the school. They've tried to spice up the gym with projections of fall leaves on the walls. The line out the door is long and full of unsteady girls on too-high heels and boys looking uncomfortably overdressed. We join the procession. I notice some of the people turning, whispering, and pointing. At me.

"I know," says Whitney to one girl standing directly in front of us. "She looks totally different, doesn't she?"

I endure the attention like some kind of doll on display.

"Wow, Whitney," says the girl. "Who would have dreamed you could do that?"

"Hey, what about me?" I finally say. They both look at me like the doll shouldn't speak.

Inside the double doors, the line snakes toward a leaf-covered arch and a waiting photographer. This is what's causing the backup. Everyone is posing for a picture. I watch the flash of smiling faces and feel a familiar tension start to rise. Photographs are going to be impossible to avoid. I wait for her comment, but Skinny stays silent. It's unsettling. My constant companion is gone.

It's different now. I'm different now. I have to keep reminding myself that until I believe it.

It's our turn for the picture. Jackson and I step under the arch. He wraps an arm around my waist and draws me in.

"Tilt your head up a little bit. Don't smile too big. Makes your cheeks look fat," Whitney coaches from the sideline. "Yes, just like that."

The camera flashes, and we're done. The next couple steps up under the arch and Jackson and I move into the room. The room is decorated with orange and red leaves hung from the ceiling and bunches of gold balloons tied on chairs. Large round tables with white sparkly tablecloths dot the area with only enough room for a dance floor. Squealing, excited girls teeter-totter across the room, wearing dresses that feature lots of sparkle and little else. Boys lean against walls, trying to look casual and cool. At the far end of the room is a stage with a drum set, piano, and guitars.

We push our way through the people, who are all talking and laughing together in dressed-up clumps. The clouds of perfume change scents as we pass each group of dressed-to-the-hilt girls, leaving me with a dull headache. Whitney keeps pushing one finger into the small of my back to keep me moving forward. I see Mr. Blair, my math teacher, and Mr. Landmann, the history teacher, talking over by the food tables. It seems strange to see teachers in suits. We finally reach an open spot over by the wall and I take a deep breath.

"Hey, there's Kristen!" Whitney squeals. She zigzags off through the crowd in her platform pumps to hug the curly-haired girl a couple of tables over.

"Want to sit down?" Jackson asks from behind me.

"Sure," I say, thinking that sitting down will probably be a little less awkward.

He speaks to Wolfgang quickly as we wind around the crowded tables, but there is no sign of Briella. Where is she? I went straight to Whitney's after school so I didn't see her, but I thought she was coming to the dance with Wolf. We finally find a couple of empty chairs at a table shaded by a fake tree with orange and yellow tissue paper leaves. I immediately take the seat nearest the wall, feeling the comfort of the little cover the tree provides. But I'm hardly sitting down before Whitney is back, with Kristen trotting along behind her.

"Wow. Remember when she broke that chair onstage last year?" Kristen calls, as Whitney drags her back to my hiding place. I wince.

"Yeah, but just wait until you see her tonight." Whitney glances over her shoulder. "She doesn't look like that at all anymore."

My hands flutter uselessly by my sides. I'm not sure what I'm supposed to be doing. Now my head and my stomach ache.

"This is what I'm talking about," Whitney announces to Kristen when they reach my side, throwing her hands wide with a flourish. "Stand up," she says to me. I get up, relunctantly.

"Surprise," I say, trying to sound funny but finding no smile to offer.

"Oh. My. God. She looks amazing." Kristen's staring at me but talking to Whitney. It's like I can't hear, and Whitney is supposed to be the translator.

"Well, she's still got a ways to go, but it's pretty dramatic," says Whitney. "Best makeover ever."

Kristen agrees enthusiastically. She smoothes her stray curls around her face and smiles encouragingly at me like I'm a dog waiting for a treat.

"You should take pictures and send them in to the Style Network or something."

"Oh, good idea," Whitney squeals. "We've already taken tons of pictures tonight."

"Look, it's Briella." Matt taps Whitney on the shoulder. We both turn and stare at the couple under the arch. "Who's that she's with?"

I look, then wish I hadn't.

"It's that guy with the weird nickname . . . Mouse?"

"Rat," I say softly.

"What is she doing with him?" Jackson asks.

"I guess it's the season for giving," Matt says with a short laugh.

"Well, I think he's cute in a geeky kind of way," says Whitney.

Watching him as the camera flashes, I have to agree. He looks adorable. His glasses are gone, replaced with the contacts his mother always wants him to wear. When he flashes that smile at the camera, those two big dimples appear right at the ideal moment and his angular face is transformed into gorgeous.

Briella is the perfect companion. Her head comes just to his shoulder, and her pink strapless dress covers her curves like Saran Wrap. The camera flashes again, catching Briella looking up at Rat with a knowing smile.

I know exactly what she's up to. It's like she's holding him hostage, with her friends as the ransom. If I give all of their attention back to her, I'll get the Rat boy back. My cheeks burn with anger. Briella doesn't really like Rat. Briella doesn't talk about him. She doesn't text him. She doesn't call him.

Or at least I don't think she does.

How did Rat get from sitting at the popular table at lunch to dating Briella? Have I been so busy with Whitney that I didn't notice what was happening between the two of them? No way.

"Want to dance?" Jackson asks me, but I shake my head.

"Not yet," I say. Briella is laughing at something Rat said.

"Okay, then I'm going to go get some punch. Want me to bring you back some?"

I smile up at him and nod. I notice he didn't offer me any food. I guess he doesn't want to undo all of Whitney's hard work. I wait for Skinny to comment, but she's still oddly silent. It should make me happy that the horrible hiss of her voice is gone, but it feels like there's an empty space in my head where she used to be, like the bloody hole that remains after you pull a tooth. Something should fill it up. I stare down at the glittery tabletop in front of me.

"Evidently you can dress me up, but you can't cover my scars," I whisper softly to no one.

Someone takes the chair beside me, and I glance up. "You look beautiful," Rat says.

"Thanks," I say. Even without his glasses, his eyes are familiar. Comforting. Everything else fades away. Whitney, Briella, Skinny. Even Jackson. Just seeing Rat makes me feel more relaxed.

"You look pretty hot yourself," I say, and he does. He pushes his bangs away from his eyes, making my stomach dip. I stare at him for a long time. Then I remember and glance around quickly.

"Where's Briella?"

"She's talking to Wolfgang," he says.

Of course she is. I see her over by the food table, laughing up at Wolf, one hand on his big, square shoulder. I turn back to face Rat, but he is looking at me. Not at Briella.

"Do you want to dance?" he murmurs, so quietly I'm sure I'm the only one who hears it.

I nod at him, wide-eyed. "I guess so," I say. My voice is nothing more than a whisper.

He stands and holds out his hand to me. I take it, and he leads me to the dance floor. When we reach the middle of the small dance space, he turns to face me very slowly until his eyes meet mine. The music is slow and familiar. "My Funny Valentine." A strange song for a high-school dance.

"I think they're playing our song," Rat says.

"You requested this?" I am trying very hard to keep my voice level.

"You said it was the most romantic Broadway song ever written when we watched that show. . . ." His voice trails off as he tries to remember the name, snapping his fingers.

"*Babes in Arms*," I say.

"That's it," he says.

He gives me a little bow and opens his arms wide, his grin full and dazzling. I don't have to be an elephant or a swan. There is no pretending. That fourth wall that Ms. DeWise is always talking about finally slides up between me and the audience. It is only the two of us on this stage.

Stepping into his arms, I put my hands on his chest, but I'm not trying to push him away. I don't have to. He already knows all the terrible secrets I've swallowed down for so long. He knows how much I weigh. It doesn't matter. I spread my fingers wide to feel the muscles under his shirt and let my hands slide up around his neck, touching the curls at his collar.

I can't resist. "*You make me smile with my heart*," I sing softly, along with the song.

I don't have to worry about his hands touching my waist or any other part of my body. It's Rat. He knows me. The real me. And it doesn't matter. I lay my head down on his shoulder in relief, and I don't flinch as he wraps his arms around me. The music is slow and we sway back and forth in time.

"How did you learn to dance?" I ask.

"YouTube videos," he says, and I laugh.

"You made it to the ball," he says. "I predicted last summer you would."

I lean back against his arms and look up. Our eyes lock. I know we're both remembering. The hospital, the weigh-ins, the exercise. I'm surprised by the feelings pulsing through my body.

"That seems like a long time ago." Ninety-nine pounds ago now and a body that has been rearranged inside to never be the same again. "I still have a long way to go," I say.

"Yes, and an audition. That will be the final step of our master plan." He fake laughs like a mad scientist. "You're going to break an arm."

My forehead crinkles in bewilderment. "You mean break a leg?"

"Whatever."

I laugh, and rest my head on his shoulder again. It feels so good to be here. I don't want it to stop. But it does.

"Can I cut in?" It's Briella, standing there in all her pink Saran Wrap glory with a stunning smile on her face. "I think your date was looking for you," she says to me. "You know . . . Jackson?"

Oh no. I forgot about Jackson, as Briella is obviously aware. She takes Rat's arm and leans into his side. How could I have forgotten about Jackson? The Prince to my Cinderella. It was just that I felt comfortable with Rat. But the truth is it didn't feel comfortable. It felt . . . amazing.

"I think he went that way." Briella gestures vaguely toward the back wall.

"I better go," I say to Rat. I can't read his expression, but the smile has vanished. He stands, tall and silent, beside Briella. They make a lovely couple.

I turn and stumble off through the crowd to the sound of Briella's laughter behind me. I'm going to kill her. Sometime tonight I'll find her and I'll confront her. She's not going to break Rat's heart just because she's jealous of all the new attention I'm getting from her friends. I won't let her. I grit my teeth and head back toward Whitney's table, but there's no sign of Jackson.

"I think I saw him a minute ago," Whitney says, when I ask her. No one else seems to know where he went, either, so I sit down at the table to wait. I can't blame Jackson for disappearing. After all, I was the one who left with Rat.

My eyes return to the dance floor and, even though I don't want to, I can't help but watch Rat and Briella dancing. It's a fast dance, and they're both laughing as they move to the music. They look like they're having fun. I blink and glance away. Everything blurs. Music. Laughter. Talking. Cinderella is at the ball, but it isn't exactly what I'd dreamed.

I listen for Skinny's voice. Still nothing.

I glance around, looking for Jackson. Prince Charming is nowhere in sight. The music stops, and Briella leaves Rat to go off toward the bathroom. Now's my chance. The music starts up again with a loud beat.

"Come on," Whitney shouts across the table. "We're all going to dance."

I shake my head. "I have to go to the bathroom," I yell over the music, and she nods. Grabbing Matt's hand, Whitney pulls him toward the dance floor, leaving behind a trail of giggling wannabes to push through the crowd and follow.

Briella is at the sink when I walk in the door.

"What are you doing?" I ask her, blocking the way out.

"What does it look like I'm doing? I'm using the bathroom."

"Like you're using Rat?"

"What are you talking about?" Briella's face gets serious. She pulls a paper towel out of the dispenser on the wall and wipes off her hands. She pushes past me to get to the trash can.

"This is about you and me. There's no reason to bring Rat into it." Anger surges through me. It makes me feel sharper and more alert. I whirl to face Briella.

She blinks at me like she doesn't know what I'm saying. But she does. I know she does.

"It isn't always about you. I like Ted," she says. "He's a good guy."

I stiffen. "Why are you calling him that?"

"I think it's time for him to leave that silly nickname behind, don't you?"

"He likes it," I say.

"Does he really? Do you even know?"

"I've asked him."

"How long ago? Fourth grade?"

I don't know how long ago it was. Could he have changed his mind and I didn't know? What else has happened without me knowing?

"He asked you to the dance, Ever," Briella says. "You were always his first choice. He told me. But you wanted to go with someone else. So why are you knocking me?"

She has a point. Not that I want to hear it. I did . . . do . . . want to be with someone else. Jackson. It's always been Jackson.

"I just don't want Rat to get hurt," I say.

"Ever," she says, "I really like him. He makes me feel smart, and funny, and something more than just pretty."

Just pretty. That's all I've wanted for so long, I don't know what else I'm supposed to want.

I realize she's telling the truth, and I don't know what's worse. Briella using Rat to get back at me or Briella actually liking Rat. My Rat. A sense of loss sweeps over me.

"I don't want you to hurt him," I mumble again.

"Why would I do that?" she asks, snapping her fingers in front of my face like she's trying to wake me up. "You really don't understand me at all, do you?"

"I guess I don't. It's not like we've exactly been friends."

"You think Whitney is your best friend now?" she asks.

"At least *she's* been nice to me." I'm not sure I really believe that, but I say it anyway.

"You think she's *nice*? You're her makeover project. It's getting her all kinds of attention. It's not about you. Don't kid yourself."

"She didn't have to do it. At least she doesn't ignore me like you do."

"You've never wanted to be friends with me. Fat or not. You've always made it clear. I'm stupid, and you can't stand me." Briella blinks quickly. Are those tears in her eyes? Because of me?

"I don't think you're stupid." I'm surprised at her anger. "I didn't mean to be that way."

"You always act like you're better than me. You think you're better than everyone. Rat doesn't act like that. He's probably a hundred times smarter than everyone in this room, but he never makes me feel dumb."

Or fat, I think, but I don't say it. I do say, "You don't understand."

"Did you ever think maybe I want to understand? And I could, too, if you would just explain it to me." Briella throws the paper towel into the trash. "I'm going back to the dance. Have fun with your new friends."

"They're your friends, too," I say.

"I'm not so sure about that," she calls back over her shoulder just before the door slams shut.

I stand, staring at the mirror for a long time after she leaves. My green eyes look sadly back at me. The only thing I recognize in the reflection. Who are my friends? Whitney? Jackson? Where were they when I weighed three hundred pounds? The music starts up again outside the bathroom walls. A soft melody. Right this minute, beautiful Briella is stepping into Rat's arms. She's where I was a few minutes ago. Right where I want to be right now.

"What do I want?" I whisper to the girl in the mirror.

A beat of silence drops into the clatter of my mind. Quiet. Not even Skinny is talking to me.

What have I done? I need to think. Stumbling out of the bathroom, I push my way through the crowd to the hallway doors. I don't want to see Briella and Rat dancing together again.

At midnight, Cinderella ran away from the ball, leaving behind her glass slipper. The doors swing slowly closed behind me, shutting out the sound of the party, and I realize I've lost something far more important than a shoe.

I've lost my best friend.

MIDNIGHT

CHAPTER NINETEEN

	Weight	Pounds Lost	Exercise	Playlist
STARTING WEIGHT: 302 HEIGHT: 5'6"				
Week 26	200	102	Dance	"The Winner Takes It All" (*Mamma Mia*)

Out in the hall, I take a couple of deep breaths, stumbling toward the junior lockers. I just need to think for a minute. The music from the dance fades away into a dull thumping in the background. I dodge a couple of giggling freshmen dragging each other back the way I just came, toward the music and the fun.

Two figures stand close to each other down by the water fountain. I blink rapidly, my mind starting to focus. Something about them is familiar. The girl is tiny. Gigi. She's wearing jeans, a long-sleeved T-shirt, and tennis shoes. She's obviously not dressed for the ball. And the boy who's standing oh-so-close to her . . . is Jackson. Their hands touch. I hear a slight buzzing in my head.

My mind is scrambled, my stomach in knots. I can't look away. God. How did this happen? When did this happen? Jackson reaches his hand around behind Gigi's neck and brings his lips down to hers. It's so easy. So natural. Like he's done it a million times before.

My heart feels like it's been wrapped in barbed wire and pushed deep inside me. I'm bleeding inside, fighting for every breath.

It's supposed to be me.

Gigi pulls back, laughing. She reaches up and brushes the hair from his eyes. Her fingers linger and then trace the line of his chin. Like I should be doing. Like I've dreamed of so many, many times. My stomach churns.

Her mouth moves, and Jackson laughs, his eyes never leaving her face. He leans in to murmur something in her hair. I can almost feel his breath on her neck. Almost. They both laugh. He pulls away, and she punches his arm playfully. It's like she hit me solidly in the stomach. I cover my mouth with my hand to try and hold in the hurt.

"You'll never be skinny enough for him." Skinny's voice fills my mind. She's back with a vengeance. In my ear. Hissing. *"Nothing is ever enough. You know that now, right?"*

Jackson leans back in toward Gigi. He's going to kiss her again, and I'm standing there like I'm watching some kind of movie. I back away into the lockers behind me, trying to get away from seeing what's coming. The clang of the metal startles them, and they jerk away from each other.

"Ever?" Jackson turns to see me standing there, but the surprise on his face is quickly replaced by guilt. "What the . . . ," Jackson says. He clears his throat.

I turn and walk blindly away from them. I'm fighting for every breath and it's not fair. Nothing matters now. Not the weight loss. Not the acting. Not the audition.

"Wait," Jackson calls. "I'll catch up with you inside," I hear him tell Gigi.

I can't walk away fast enough in these stupid high heels, and he catches up with me before I can turn the corner.

"Ever, please don't go. Let me explain," he says, touching my arm. "It was rude to be with Gigi when I came with you. I'm sorry."

"What do you have to do to make him love you?"

"Don't say you're sorry. Say I'm dreaming. Say I'm crazy. Tell me how I can change things." I realize I'm shouting. I take a deep, shaky breath, and my voice drops to a whisper. "How can I change me . . . any more?"

He closes his eyes for a minute, rubbing his fists against the closed lids. Then opens them. "It's not you." He says the thing everyone says when they break someone's heart.

"Of course it's you." Skinny's voice is gloating in my ear.

Jackson shakes his head. "It was Whitney. She likes you, and she wanted you to have a chance to go to the ball." His voice trails off as his eyes meet mine. "She thought you deserved to have a good time."

"He only feels pity for you. They all do."

Shame washes over me.

"Whitney doesn't *like* me. She just wanted a fix-up project and you're the perfect accessory." I smile bitterly.

"This thing with Gigi . . . it all just happened. I'd already asked you and I didn't want to hurt your feelings. . . ." He gestures toward the gym door. ". . . Or make Whitney mad."

Jackson is a coward. "Please leave," I whisper. "Please just leave."

He walks toward the open gym doors and the music. I stand there watching him leave and know I should be doing something. Walking away. Something.

"Wait," he says, turning back to face me. "Why did you stop?"

"Stop what?"

"Liking me."

"Why do you think that?" I ask, confused.

"We were friends. More than friends. You kissed me. Then everything stopped." He shrugs with embarrassment. "I just wondered what happened. You started looking at me like . . . you hated me."

"He's lying. He's the one who stopped liking you. Remember?"

"Just like the look you're giving me." He points at my face. "Like you can't stand anything about me."

I didn't hate him. Far from it. I hated the voice I heard in my head. Skinny's voice. But Skinny was the one who told me the truth, right?

"I never stopped liking you," I say quietly.

"Then why did you stop calling? Why did you stop coming over?"

"Because you're fat and ugly. Nobody likes someone like you."

I try to focus. Skinny's voice is talking over Jackson's. I can't listen to them both at the same time. They are saying different things. One of them is lying. But which one?

"I tried to talk to you a couple of times. But it was like you couldn't hear me," Jackson says.

"And now you like Gigi," I say.

"Yeah," he says, looking me directly in the eyes. "I do. I'm sorry."

Don'tcrydon'tcrydon'tcry. I look down at the tips of my fancy pointed black shoes, blinking frantically. No glass slippers, just a glass heart shattering into a million slivers of regret. This isn't the way the fairy tale is supposed to end. Everyone knows that.

"Alone. Alone. Alone," Skinny chants in my ear.

Jackson puts a hand on my shoulder, and I look up. I search his face for the boy I walked with through the snow, but he's gone. He's been gone for a very long time. Maybe he never even existed. Prince Charming is just a character in a childish fairy tale of my own making.

His mouth is moving, but I can't hear what he's saying. The chanting is so loud. I concentrate. Focus.

"Are you going to be okay?" Jackson asks me again.

"Sure," I say, because what does it matter if I say something different?

"Gigi and I never meant to hurt you."

"Oh, brother! Like that's supposed to make you feel better?" Skinny yells in my right ear. I wince, and Jackson frowns down at me.

"I should go," he says. I nod, and he leaves me standing alone in the empty hallway. All my plans. Gone.

Stupid. Stupid. Stupid. I walk away down the hall, my head feeling disconnected from my body. The music and laughter from the party inside the gym seems far away, like a television left on in a different room.

CHAPTER TWENTY

I stagger through an open door. It's the theater. The place where I'm supposed to have my biggest triumph. I stumble down one of the side aisles toward the front of the stage, sinking into one of the seats in the first row. The lights are all on, but I'm in the dark.

I should laugh, really. It's funny, right? Jackson liked me all along, and I threw it away. I screwed everything up by myself. And then I went and did all this, thinking I could win him back. The surgery. The new clothes and hair. The drama class. Everything. For what?

"You are still fat and ugly. None of it mattered. You don't matter." Skinny is here, too, and she isn't whispering. Her voice echoes through the empty auditorium.

"You will always be alone. Your father has Charlotte. Your mother is gone. There is no one for you."

It was never about Jackson. I was in love with a memory, so unreal and fleeting it doesn't even matter anymore. The truth slashes into my mind. It is about me . . . and Skinny. I shake my head, trying to clear my thoughts. Skinny is haunting me like a ghost, chasing after me like a shadow. She won't quit saying her horrible words, her lips to my ear.

"Stop." My voice is shaking, the tears flowing freely from the edges of my eyes. I'm standing on a cliff, the rest of the world beneath me. I'm broken and I'm never going to heal. I cry until my throat is empty.

Skinny is waiting just offstage. Behind the curtain. I feel her. I hear her breathing there in shallow little horrible rasps. She's farther away, but her voice is even stronger. Unmistakable. She's no longer tiny and fluttering around to whisper in my ear. Solid and life-sized, she's standing just behind that stage curtain. A shiver of fear runs up the nape of my neck.

"If only you were skinny like Gigi. Then he would love you," Skinny hisses from offstage. *"But you will never look like her."*

Her whispers crawl around inside my dress. I swallow, hard. The truth is I could have had everything. I lost Rat to Briella, and I ruined things with Jackson. It wasn't about Gigi. I did it. It wasn't anyone else's fault. Skinny has it all wrong, but she's not listening.

"You're a hippo. A fat cow. An elephant!"

She's yelling now so loudly I can't hear anything else. I clap my hands over my ears and lower my head to my knees. Shutting my eyes tightly, I breathe carefully in and out, in and out. For a moment, all I can hear is my own breathing. Like I'm underwater. Or already buried deep underground. Six feet under.

"Stop it," I whisper, but she refuses to listen.

"Fat. Huge. Ugly. Hideous. Pitiful. Alone," she chants.

I open my eyes and stand, facing the darkness waiting there in the shadows of the stage.

"Shut up," I say louder, but my words come out through gritted teeth. My hands are clenched tightly at my sides. It's now or never.

"Come out here where I can see you." My voice is stronger now as I wipe the tears away from my cheeks with the back of one hand. She can't stay in the dark anymore. It's time we came face-to-face.

"Come out, come out wherever you are," Skinny chants softly.

"I want to see who . . . what . . . you are." I walk up to the front of the stage, waiting. My pulse jumps wildly in my throat.

"You don't need to see me. Just listen." Skinny's voice comes from the shadows. *"You're a big, gigantic whale. Listen. . . ."*

Wait. Something huge and powerful stirs in my brain. Like an elephant charging out of the jungle. Everything is changing except for Skinny. She's been my one constant — the nagging fairy godmother whose voice led me down this path.

"Elephants don't back down," I say, "and I'm not afraid to see you." Slowly, with my thoughts, I pull her out into the light and onto the stage. And I see her.

Finally.

My mouth falls open in surprise. She doesn't look like some cool, goth Tinker Bell. She is me. But not me. I blink to clear my eyes, but the image doesn't focus. It's like looking into one of those warped mirrors in a fun house. Her mouth is slack, no sign of emotion. Her eyes stay fixed on the floor. I put my hand out into the space in front of me and she ripples away like touched water. She still doesn't look up at me, her eyes hidden beneath lowered lids, but the shadowy figure mirrors my movement.

"Your arms are so fat they shake when you point to something," Skinny says, but it is a soft voice that twists away into the air. I can barely hear it.

"You aren't looking at me," I say, and she starts to blur even more, her edges spinning away into the dark space of the stage. "How do you even know what I look like?"

She is silent.

"Look at me!" I command her. "Tell me what you see."

Slowly, she raises her head, and the monster steps out of the closet. Her eyes are opaque and milky white with no life behind them. I clap my hand over my mouth to keep from screaming.

Skinny is blind.

"You lie!" I choke on the words. The realization makes my head spin. Skinny bases everything on appearance, all her horrible whispers, but the truth is, she can't see anything at all.

"You lie," she mimics back to me in a singsong voice, but she keeps crumbling away, breaking into pieces. I can see through her to the other side. She is nothing.

"Stop it. Stop. *STOP!*" I yell at the disintegrating creature in front of me. "It's your turn to listen to me. I'm done believing what you say. I'm so much more than what you've made me."

"You made me," she echoes. Her voice is shaky, confused, but

for once I hear the truth. If I made her, then I can change her . . . me. There's a crack there. I have to push harder. I've been the one feeding Skinny all along, but now it's time for me to make the choice. Her or the rest of my life?

"I am a good person. I can sing beautifully," I say carefully. "I am . . . pretty."

"Well, you are thinner than you were." Her voice sounds hesitant.

That's right. I can change. What. She. Says.

"I am pretty. Say it." I point at her with a shaking finger.

"You look okay in the dress."

"No, I look *pretty*. Say it."

But she can't say anything because, just like that, the fading image in front of me flickers and vanishes. It's time for the princess to say good-bye to her fairy godmother. Skinny isn't standing on center stage, or sitting on my shoulder, or talking in my ear. Skinny only exists inside my own head. She is part of me, but she's only one part. There's also an elephant part of me that is big and proud. And a singer part of me that people would love to hear. And a daughter part of me that misses her mother and loves her father. And maybe, there's a friend part of me, too.

I need to talk to Briella.

CHAPTER TWENTY-ONE

H ow was the dance?"

My dad is waiting up when I get home, sitting in a chair with his reading glasses on, but there's no book in sight. "You're home early."

"The limo driver gave me a ride. Whitney's dad paid him for the whole night, so he was just waiting around," I say.

Dad's eyebrows rise in question. I'm not ready to talk about it just yet, so I change the subject. "Any weird criminal news? I could use a smile right about now."

"Walter Johnson crashed the La-Z-Boy chair he converted into a motorized vehicle — complete with stereo and cupholders — into a car outside Lurlene's Lounge."

"He really got it to move?"

"Oh, definitely," Dad says. "It was powered by a lawn-mower motor and had a steering wheel, headlights, and even an antenna."

"Impressive." I kick the high heels off and lean over to rub one aching bare foot.

Dad continues, "Walter's not arguing the fact he was 'extremely drunk,' he just wants his La-Z-Boy back."

"Well, he did go to a lot of trouble." I finally smile.

"Ahhh. There it is. That looks better," Dad says and pats the chair beside him. "Come sit down and tell me all about it."

"The dance was okay," I say.

"That doesn't sound too wonderful. What happened, peanut?"

"Oh, Dad." I squeeze into the big, overstuffed chair beside him, and he puts his arm around me. "Things just didn't turn out the way I thought they would."

He pulls me in a little tighter but doesn't ask for any more explanation. After a few minutes he says, "When one door closes, another one opens."

I laugh. "That's what Mom used to always say."

He smiles and pats my shoulder. "She'd be so proud of you. You know that, right?"

"I hope so." We sit there, both remembering. "Sometimes I just wish I could see her, and I want her to look happy. Not like she looked the last time I saw her," I say, before I have time to think. The sadness washes over his face, and I'm sorry the minute that long-unspoken wish comes out of my mouth.

"You always made us both so, so happy," he says, blinking rapidly from behind his reading glasses. "And that's always what we wanted for you . . . happiness."

"I know, Dad," I say, patting his leg. "Don't worry. I'll get there."

I rest my head on his shoulder, and we sit like that for a while, not talking. His arm feels good.

"That dance must have been a real dud for everyone. Briella's home early, too." Dad finally breaks the silence.

"She's home?" I ask, surprised, and he nods. "I need to talk to her." I struggle to get out of the deep chair, but I lean back over to kiss Dad on the forehead.

"Night, peanut," he says.

I don't go straight upstairs. I need a moment to think about what I want to say to Briella. Maybe a glass of water will buy me the time I need to figure it out.

When I enter the kitchen, Charlotte is sitting alone at the table drinking a steaming cup of coffee.

She glances up at me. "Want me to make you something?" she asks.

"No," I say, getting a glass down out of the cabinet. I glance over at her while I'm filling it up with water from the front of the fridge. She stares straight ahead, sipping the coffee silently.

"Everything okay?" I ask, sitting down in the chair across the table from her.

She sniffs loudly. "I'm just being silly," she says. "She's fine, you know."

I nod like I know what's she's talking about, but when she glances across at my face she must realize I'm confused.

"I miss Lindsey. She called tonight from school," Charlotte

says, putting her lipstick-stained mug down on the table. "She said she might stay on campus over the summer. Take some summer classes."

"Summer's a long time away. You never know. Things can change."

"She's so busy with everything. She might even get a part-time job."

"That's a good thing, right?" I ask.

"Yes," she says, but it doesn't sound like she believes it. "She's so grown-up. It seems like yesterday she was just a baby. Such a beautiful, happy child. Always laughing. Always making everyone else smile. She grew up so fast and now she's gone."

"She's not gone. She's just not here." I'm surprised at the despair on Charlotte's face. Lindsey's just away at college. She's three hours away. It's not like it's forever.

"You don't understand." Charlotte stirs her coffee. "She left me," she finally says. "It's not just about going to college. She's been so distant for so long."

Lindsey and I never talked much, but if I had the chance now I'd tell her that moms are a very hard thing to lose. "She'll be back," I say, and pat Charlotte's hand awkwardly on the tabletop, searching for the right words of comfort. "For Christmas and weekends."

"It won't be the same." Charlotte smiles sadly. "She'll never *live* here again."

I realize I never knew Lindsey enough to miss her. Charlotte never knew my mom, either, but we are both grieving.

"I'm sure she misses you, too," I say. "She's just too cool to admit it."

Charlotte beams at me. By her expression, you'd have thought I'd given her a thousand-dollar shopping spree to Macy's. I feel guilty and make a mental note: Be nicer to Charlotte. We have some things in common.

"Thanks, Ever. I needed to talk to someone." She stands to put the empty mug in the sink.

"Sure," I say. "Anytime." Hearing Charlotte seems a little easier without Skinny's constant voice in my head.

Upstairs, I knock on the partially open door, making it swing into the room a few more inches. Briella lies on her bed, texting on her phone. Roxanne is on the pillow beside her. Both of them look up at me at the same time. Briella's blond hair is scraped back into a ponytail and the only sign of the dance is the pile of pink dress on the floor by the bed. Her face is scrubbed clean, but her eyes are red and puffy. She's been crying.

"Can I come in?" I stand in the doorway, shifting from one foot to the other. She could say no. I wouldn't blame her.

"Yeah," she says, and puts the phone over on her nightstand. I'm not sure what Briella's thinking, but Roxanne looks really sad. She thumps her tail once in greeting.

"Why is Rox in here?" I ask.

"She's in trouble. She ate half of Charlotte's Chinese silk scarf and turned the couch pillow into feather confetti," says Briella, "but she's really sorry."

Roxanne thumps her tail twice in agreement, dislodging one lone feather, then puts her head back down on the pillow with a woeful sigh. Briella brushes away any remaining sign of tears, but we both know they were there minutes before.

"What do you want?" she asks.

"Can I sit down?"

Briella pats her bed in response, and I sit. I don't know where to start.

"Are you all right?" I ask.

"I'm fine." She bites her bottom lip, her eyes darting over to the phone on the nightstand. "My dad isn't coming on Saturday. He just texted me. Not a big surprise."

"I'm sorry, Bri. He's the one missing out."

She looks at me like she's trying to tell if I'm being sincere or not. I can't blame her.

"I know how you feel," I say, but nobody really knows how anyone else feels. I know that now. "I mean, not exactly, but . . . I miss my mom. Every single day. And I wish she was here in my life, like you wish your dad was here."

"Your mom didn't leave you on purpose." Briella stares at a spot on the bedspread in front of her.

"No, but I still know what it feels like to lose your parent. No one can fix it, and I'm really sorry."

"I thought when I moved in we'd be friends, but you never wanted that." Me, friends with Briella? That's what she wanted? Listening to Skinny all these years has cost me more than I ever knew.

"I've been selfish and . . . blind," I say quietly. What a hypocrite. I felt like nothing, but I made everything all about me. I looked at the world around me through Skinny's unseeing white, opaque eyes. Including Briella. "I didn't see what you were going through. You were here in the same house, and I didn't even know."

Briella raises her pale blue eyes, bright with unshed tears, to meet mine. I watch one single tear slip out and slide down her cheek, but she doesn't try to hide it this time. Her eyes search my face and, when she finds the truth she's searching for, her shoulders relax. I finally see a small, crooked smile.

"Thanks," she says, twisting a strand of her long hair around and around one finger. "So, what happened at the dance?"

"Jackson doesn't love me." I dive right in, my voice pinched and tight.

"I know," she says. "I'm sorry."

I guess everyone knew but me.

Briella takes a breath, and looks over at me. "You can't make someone love you. No matter what you do." Something about the way she says it makes me think she's not just talking about me and Jackson. It's about her father, too.

"I did it all for him," I say, but now I'm not sure.

"Did you?" she asks. I have no idea what she is talking about.

Or maybe I do. This isn't about Jackson anymore.

"It's okay if you like Rat," I say, but the words hurt coming out. It's definitely not okay.

"That's good," she says, "because I do like him. He's smart and kind."

"I know," I say, feeling like my heart is being chewed up by Roxanne.

"And funny." Okay, just keep kicking me when I'm down.

"And he likes me, too. He never makes me feel stupid."

"You're not stupid, Briella."

"I want to believe that," she says, "but sometimes there's this voice in my head that tells me something different. Know what I mean?"

Her eyes meet mine.

"Yeah," I say. "I do."

"What happened with Jackson?" she asks.

"He likes Gigi," I say, and she nods. "Why didn't you tell me?"

"You were so happy about the dance and all. I didn't want to ruin it for you."

I can't believe this is Briella. She's full of surprises. Skinny's lies kept me from seeing the real person behind the pretty face. How did I miss what was right there in front of me all along?

"The dance didn't make me happy," I say, but then I remember dancing with Rat and feeling better than I'd ever imagined feeling. Now that's gone, too.

"So, you and Rat?" I ask.

"Rat would be a great boyfriend. . . ."

"But?"

"He doesn't think of me that way. We're just friends." She smiles gently at me like I'm a little child. "Besides, he likes me, but he doesn't *love* me. He's crazy about someone else."

"Who?" I ask, in a small voice. IhopeIhopeIhope.

"Oh, Ever, sometimes for being so smart, you are incredibly dumb." She laughs. "Rat's in love with you. He's always been in love with you. You're the only one who can't see it."

The heat rushes to my cheeks. Rat's in love with me. I could hear it a million times and never get tired of it. Could it actually be true? I want to believe it so bad.

"And now I've messed it up." My voice sounds like it's coming from way far away.

"Maybe not. Rat has stuck with you through a lot. He's not the type of guy to disappear when things get rough." Briella reaches down to scratch Roxanne's dark head, and Roxanne immediately stretches out onto her side for a tummy rub. "You should talk to him."

"I will," I say, but I don't know what I'll say.

"So what about the audition? The musical tryout is coming up, right?"

"It was."

"Was?" She squints at me.

"I don't know if I want to go through with it now. The last time I was on a stage in front of a lot of people . . ." My voice trails off at the memory of sitting on top of that broken chair.

"A lot has changed since then. You've changed."

"Maybe I haven't changed enough."

"So, you want to give up?" She places both hands on her knees and leans in to stare intently into my eyes.

"It's not giving up," I say, but I know it really is.

"Do you want to be on a stage singing for people? Do you

want a part in the musical?" She considers me for a moment, and then hits me hard with the last question. "Do you still *want* it?"

"Yeah," I say, without even pausing to think about it. "I do." My answer surprises me, but as I say it, I know it's true.

"Then all of this wasn't for Jackson. It was for you."

I think about it. "Yes, it was."

"Then get up on that stage and show them what you can do. You're going to wow them."

"Look at you. Being all cheerleader."

"God, no." She laughs. "Don't ever call me that."

I rub Roxanne's tummy, and she stretches her head back on the pillow in ecstasy. "You know, I always thought Rat would be in the audience during the audition," I say. "Now I'm not so sure he'll want to be."

"You should ask him," Briella says. A little hope unfurls somewhere deep inside me. "That might be all he's waiting for."

"I don't know if I can," I say doubtfully. "What about you? Will you come?"

"You want me to be there?"

I nod, and she claps her hands together, startling a short bark out of Roxanne, who hops down off the bed, ready for something exciting to happen.

Briella leans over and hugs me. "I'll be your biggest fan," she says softly over my shoulder, and I laugh because it is so different from the voice I usually hear whispering in my ear.

EVER AFTER

CHAPTER TWENTY-TWO

	Weight	Pounds Lost	Exercise	Playlist
STARTING WEIGHT: 302 HEIGHT: 5'6"				
Week 26	198	104	Run/Walk 3 miles	"Listen" (*Dreamgirls*)

Briella drives me to the audition and walks in with me. People are spread out in individual seats throughout the auditorium, but there's a pretty good crowd. The audition is open to anyone who wants to listen, but I recognize quite a few kids from drama class, including Kristen Rogers, who is sitting in the second row, literally biting her nails. I see Gigi and Jackson near the front left-hand side of the stage, his arm draped across the back of her shoulders. She smiles up at him, and he tucks a strand of blue hair behind one ear. I wait for the jolt of jealousy to hit, but it doesn't.

"What happened to you at the Ball?" Whitney stands in front of us with her two hands placed firmly on her hips, blocking the way to the seats. "One minute you were dancing and the next you were nowhere to be found. Jackson said you left."

"I wasn't feeling well."

"Was it your stomach?" she asks. Her brow wrinkles and her eyes narrow.

"Just forget it," Briella says. She grabs one of my arms and tries to pull me around Whitney. "Let's go. It's going to start in a minute."

"Wait. Was it . . ." Whitney's voice lowers and she grabs my other arm to keep us from leaving. She looks around quickly to see who might be nearby and then whispers dramatically, "Dumping?"

"No," I say. "It wasn't anything like that."

"Because I told Jackson that punch was way too sweet." Whitney is rigid, her eyes unwavering. "I should have known."

She's concerned? About me?

"It wasn't that," I say quickly.

Briella rolls her eyes, but I pull my arm out of her grasp. I feel like I need to say something.

"I'm sorry about the dance, Whitney. You went to a lot of trouble," I say. "I know you wanted it all to be special."

"I did." Her lower lip sticks out and quivers just a bit. She glances over at Briella. "I *really* did."

She's not going to actually cry, is she? Oh, God. I can't leave the powerful, popular Whitney Stone looking like that. Even Briella looks a little taken aback.

"You did an amazing job," I say, patting Whitney's shoulder. "I never thought I could look like that in a million years. It felt wonderful."

The auditorium lights blink on and off.

"I have to go," I say to Whitney. "We'll talk later, okay?"

"Okay." She sniffs once, straightens, and throws her hair back over one shoulder. The Whitney Stone I know is back in an instant. The curtain of perfection drops to cover her emotions, and I'm left wondering if I ever actually saw it in the first place.

Briella pulls me away from Whitney and toward the aisle leading up to the stage.

"This is for you," Briella says, and pushes something into my hand. "Go ahead and sit up front. I have a seat saved for me right in the middle. You'll see me."

"Wish me luck," I say, reaching out to grab her hand.

"I've heard you sing. You don't need luck," she says, and gives my hand a quick squeeze.

Three people sit about ten rows from the front with clipboards and pens. One of them is Ms. DeWise, her red hair tied up with a yellow ribbon into a massive curly knot of escaping frizzy corkscrews. I think the balding man with the green bow tie is the choir teacher, and the other one is a girl with shoulder-length black hair who barely looks older than me. Maybe some former high-school theater star? I'm not sure. They all look serious, heads together, talking in whispers as they flip through the papers in their laps.

I hold on to a small piece of folded paper Briella slipped into my hand a few minutes ago. Then I start to plan where I can sit — where there's room for me — in these small, folding auditorium seats. Then I remember. I can fit anywhere now. I slide into the seat next to Kristen, and she glances over with her index finger still in her mouth. She spits out a bite of nail and keeps chewing.

"Congratulations," I say. Even the butterflies in my stomach can't keep me from noticing the space between me and Kristen. "You decided to go through with it."

"I think I'm going to throw up."

"No, you're not. Take some deep breaths."

She takes her finger out of her mouth and breathes in and out obediently. I notice her left leg is jumping up and down like it's disconnected from the rest of her body.

"Relax. You're going to do fine." I lay my hand on her knee and push down on her leg to stop the jerking. "What's your monologue?"

"It's from *Guys and Dolls*." She clenches her fists together in her lap, digging her fingers into her palms to keep from being able to access her nubby, well-chewed nails. "My mom hates it when I bite my nails. What are you doing?"

"It's a piece from *Beauty and the Beast*."

"Beauty?"

"No, the Beast." I grin at her. "I can relate to the part."

"Why?" Kristen looks confused. Although I'm surprised she doesn't get it, I don't explain. She asks, "Do you think we sing first or do the monologue first?"

"I don't know," I say. "This is my first audition."

"Me, too," she says, her clenched fists now tapping on her shaking knees.

Shocker. Somehow I've figured that out.

The stage is empty except for a piano and the accompanist, who is ruffling through the selection of music they handed her a few minutes before. One spotlight circles center stage front. Waiting. I swallow once. Twice. I. Can. Do. This.

I open my fist and stare down at the tiny piece of paper neatly folded into a perfect square. Slowly, I open it and stare down at a tiny picture. It's an intricate pencil drawing of a mouse. Not a cartoony mouse with cute, human-like features, but a scientifically perfect sketch of the species. There's no mistaking Rat's handiwork. This mouse will go perfectly with the pumpkin on my bedroom wall. I smile down at the tiny picture and the butterflies in my stomach land for a minute, their wings stilled. Glancing up quickly from the paper, my eyes search the seats until I see Briella and Rat sitting near the middle of the center row.

He came. Even though I didn't — couldn't — ask him. He flashes me a brilliant Rat grin and lifts a hand in salute. He's here. Watching. And knowing that makes me smile, too. I wave back, the scrap of paper fluttering in my hand. I want him to know I got it and that I knew it was from him. I turn back to the stage and inhale deeply. I'm going to do this.

The first name called is Chance Lehmann. His mop of curly brown hair is stuffed under a top hat, and he sings from *Les Misérables*. It's not bad, but he really has to stretch for the high notes. Then he recites a monologue from *Bye Bye Birdie*, and the audience laughs at all the right spots. With his sexy smile, he'd make a great Prince Charming. I try to imagine him singing directly to me, all eyes on me, and feel heat flush up my cheeks. The applause is enthusiastic as he walks back to his seat, waving to the crowd. I glance back over my shoulder for the judges' expressions. Bow-Tie Man smiles as he writes notes on his pad, and the other two are deep in conversation.

Kristen is called next. For a minute, I don't think she's going to get out of her seat.

"You can do this," I whisper, and give her a push to get started.

She stumbles up the stairs and to the microphone.

"Tell us about yourself," Ms. DeWise says.

"I can tell you that I'm really scared to be here," says Kristen, and the audience laughs. She looks surprised at the reaction, but that's all it really takes. After a few minutes, and a quick monologue and song, she's practically running back to her seat. Her face is flushed with excitement and her curls bounce with every step.

We slap high five as she sits down beside me again. "Good job!" I whisper.

My name is called, and I go up the side steps to the stage. I look back over my shoulder for Briella and Rat. My stepsister waves and gives a thumbs-up. I stop mid-step. Rat nods his head slowly, up and down, encouraging me. This is it. I step up onto the stage.

Walking slowly into the spotlight, the audience is instantly blacked out. I take a deep breath in and let it out slowly.

"I don't think I've seen you here before . . . Ms. Davies. Are you new to this school?" I recognize the disembodied voice as the bow-tied choir teacher.

"No," I say.

"Have you been involved in our choral program?"

"No."

"How about theater? Taken any classes?"

"Yes," I say. "One."

"Tell us about yourself." This time it's Ms. DeWise's voice.

I clear my throat. I'm going to say something I've never said in my whole life. Something I've been terrified to tell anyone.

"My name is Ever Davies, and this time last year I weighed three hundred and two pounds."

There is a long silence from the blackness behind the lights. I start talking, but it's not the monologue I'd planned from *Beauty and the Beast*. It's something altogether different and unrehearsed, but it pours out of me as though I'd practiced it for years.

"I've lost over a hundred pounds, and there's no one in this room who can play Cinderella like I can. You might think I don't look like a princess, but she and I have a lot in common.

Look at me." I raise my arms from my sides and turn around slowly in the spotlight. I welcome all the eyes. "Take a good look. You see, Cinderella and I know what it's like to look in the mirror and not recognize the reflection. We know what it's like to change."

I face the audience again. It's so quiet behind the lights, I almost think there's no one there. Then comes the sound of someone nervously clearing a throat. They're all still out there, waiting for what I'm going to say next.

I lean in to speak directly into the microphone. "I've learned a few things about being a real-life Cinderella, though. Sometimes a prince isn't that easy to recognize. And everyone has good parts and bad parts to them, no matter how good or bad they may seem on the outside. Cinderella isn't all good, and the stepsister . . ." I wish I could see Briella in the audience. "The stepsister isn't all bad."

The silence stretches out again, and I wait. I hear the slight rustle of restless movement beyond the footlights, and I think about who is listening to me and watching me from the rows of seats. Even though I can't see them now, I know exactly where they are. On the left is the sophomore boy who made oinking sounds every time I walked down the hall; in the center is Tracey, the girl whose big speech I interrupted by breaking a chair with my huge body. At the back is my new "BFF," Whitney, who believes I owe all my newfound popularity to her. Gigi is sitting with Jackson three rows in front of her, holding hands. Then, of course, there's Briella and Rat.

Ms. DeWise finally speaks. "Anything else?"

"Yes," I say, "I'm a really good singer."

Finally, the choir teacher asks, "So what are you going to sing for us today?"

"'Listen' from *Dreamgirls*," I say. I picked the song carefully. I knew what I wanted to say. I knew exactly what would take away the jitters. I just had to sing it.

"Start whenever you're ready."

I take a second. Shut my eyes and focus. Then I nod for the pianist to the start the introduction. The piano begins to play, and I come in a little late, but I catch up quickly. The pianist is good, which helps. She slows to match my pace.

I stand very still. No choreography. I let the music fill up my body and my mind. The lyrics are engrained in my brain. I don't think about them. It's time. I start to sing, and I feel the wave of audience response come over the stage toward me. It's happening. I hit the first high note. Clear, pitch-perfect. It's the only thing I do that's effortless. Weightless. The music opens the door, and everything in me that could be possible pours out. It is my anthem.

> *"I followed the voice*
> *you gave to me*
> *But now I gotta find, my own . . ."*

This is what the surgery was all about. Nobody is laughing at me or calling me names. Not even the voice deep inside.

I don't sing for the three judges out front. I don't even sing for the scattered students, my competition, in the audience.

I sing for Skinny.

The music swells. It feels like a plug is pushing into the socket, and I connect with everyone sitting in every chair. I will never be viewed the same again. Not by myself and not by anyone sitting in this room.

CHAPTER TWENTY-THREE

"**Y**ou were amazing!" Briella waits outside the auditorium doors with a huge grin on her face. She grabs my shoulders and pulls me in for an enthusiastic hug.

"Thanks." I can hardly get that one word out. She's squeezing me so tight and spinning me around and jumping up and down all at the same time. It feels like I've been dropped in a blender with the top off.

When the spinning, jumping, and hugging finally stop, I manage to ask, "So, you think it went okay?"

She bursts into laughter. "You dope, it was so much better than okay. And you know it."

She is right. I do know it. I was terrific. My smile feels like it's going to break open my face.

"Where's Rat?" I ask Briella.

"He's outside waiting for you."

I mumble something under my breath.

"What?" Briella asks.

"I'm scared," I say again, but this time it comes out much stronger.

"After what you just did, *this* is what scares you?" Briella asks, incredulously.

"I've got more to lose with this."

"Just go talk to him. He's outside."

I push open the metal doors and walk out into the cool night air. Rat is sitting with his back to me over on the stone benches around the flagpole. When I walk up behind him, he doesn't turn.

"Did you get the part?" Rat asks.

"I don't know yet. I think it'll be posted tomorrow down by the choir room." I walk around in front of the bench to face him.

"You will," Rat says, finally looking up at me. His face is still, but I can see a muscle in his cheek jumping. "All evidence points to that outcome."

"So, you want to talk?" I ask hesitantly. I stand with my arms crossed across my chest, waiting for his response.

"Sure," he says, and pats the empty spot beside him. I sit down on the cold bench and stare off across the parking lot. He sits quietly next to me. I can feel his eyes on my face. I pause, taking a deep breath.

Finally, I blurt, "I miss you and me." I twist around on the bench to face him. "I know I've done some stupid things lately, and I'm really sorry, and you probably think I'm horrible."

"I don't think you're horrible at all." He turns, his knees

touching mine. "I think you needed to figure out what you wanted. Who you wanted."

"I've figured it out." I reach out to touch his shoulder, my hand sliding down the side of his arm until it rests on the top of his hand. "I couldn't have done any of it without you."

"Yes, you could have." He turns his hand over, cupping my hand in his, fingers sliding between mine. It feels like coming home.

"I need you." It comes out weird and intense sounding.

He slowly leans across my body, his lips inches from mine. "I need you, too, Ever."

Then he kisses me, and it's not a Cinderella and Prince Charming kiss. Nothing like that. It's a Sleeping Beauty kiss. A kiss that jolts every nerve in my body that has been sleeping for hundreds of years. Everything comes screaming awake. All I can do is feel. Feel his lips and his tongue and his arms and his heart all together at once. I feel every touch, every taste, every everything. I finally understand what it's like to be truly awake, and I never ever want to go back to sleep again.

"You know, the odds are I probably won't ever be skinny," I say, when the kissing finally stops for a few moments.

"I loved you when you were three hundred and two pounds, and I love you now." His gaze locks with mine.

He loves me. He *loves* me. He loves *me*. I want him to say it again and again and again.

"I love you, too," I say. I know he already knows it. He's probably known it for a long time. He's smart like that.

"That's good to hear," Rat says.

"Do you love me *more* now?" I ask. Because I'm prettier and thinner and more popular and . . .

"Probably less," he says, matter-of-factly. I lean away from him in mock surprise, but his arms keep me from going far. "The percentage of affection in proportion to pounds weighed results in less of you to love."

I sock him in the arm, pushing him away. "Seriously? You're going to get all scientific on me now?"

"Ouch," he says, holding on to his shoulder like I really hurt him. "My theory is I'm going to love you even if you're skinny."

"Why?" I slide my hand back into the warmth of his, leaning my head down until it rests on his shoulder. I want to hear his reasons. After all, he always has data to support his conclusions, right? I think he might say I'm smart and brave and talented. And I think I know now I'm all those things, but he says something else. Something that's new for me to hear.

"Because you are, and have always been, beautiful."

CHAPTER TWENTY-FOUR

	Weight	Pounds Lost	Exercise	Playlist
STARTING WEIGHT: 302 HEIGHT: 5'6"				
Week 35	185	117	Choreography	"I'm Here" (*The Color Purple*)

"You should see the crowd out there. I can't see a single empty seat." Kristen is panting with excitement.

"You looked?" I turn in my chair, pushing the full skirt of my costume to the side.

"How else would I know?"

"Huge taboo. Theater bad luck." Chance says, then meets my eyes in the mirror and winks. He's sitting beside me in a makeshift dressing room and has been torturing Kristen like this for weeks now. "Now you have to turn around three times, kiss your pinkie finger, and touch the stage floor to ward off the bad karma."

"Is he kidding me?" Kristen turns to me for support.

"Don't look at me. Evidently, he's the expert," I say.

"It's a total theater thing," he says.

Kristen nods so enthusiastically the mouse ears on her head almost fly off. She starts turning around slowly and counting out loud.

"You've got to stop this," I say to Chance, while Kristen spins around behind me. "She'll be exhausted before the first act."

"She likes it," he says. "Besides, it helps with the nerves."

There's a rustle and a lot of movement behind me, but I can't turn around because Whitney, who shocked the popular crowd by enlisting as drama makeup tech, is putting the final puff of powder on my face. Volunteering to be in charge of hair and makeup for the production definitely put her evil genius to good use. She says it will all go into her stylist portfolio.

"Sit still," she grumbles.

"Full house!" Briella's smiling face pops into the mirror behind a scowling Whitney. She waves a big bouquet of daisies and roses into my line of sight. "We're in the third row back on your right-hand side. The empty seat is for your dad. He's on his way, so don't panic."

"Something wrong?" I ask.

"No big deal. Randy Marchet tried to rob the Huntsville National Bank. He disguised his face using permanent markers, so he was pretty easy to spot at the Sonic down the street." She leans over my shoulder, ignoring Whitney's glare, and puts the bouquet of flowers on the tabletop in front of me. "These are from your dad."

Whitney gives up fussing over me with a sigh. "That's the best I can do for now. Don't mess it up before curtain."

"Can I have more eyeliner?" Chance begs.

"You already look like a pirate now," Whitney says, but she moves over to his side. "Look up toward the ceiling," she commands.

Briella moves around where I can see her better. "Are you ready?"

"I have to be, don't I?"

"Nervous?"

"A little bit," I answer. Maybe more than a little bit.

She leans forward to cup my face in her hands, looking intently into my eyes. "It will all go away once you step out on that stage."

"I hope you're right."

"I have something else for you." She leans back to push her hand deep into her blue jean pocket. I look down in surprise at the gift in the palm of her hand. The tiny silver box is tied with an unusual color of blue ribbon. I remember the color from Rat's stained fingertips — indigo.

"Take it. He wants you to open it now," Briella says, holding out her hand.

Picking up the box carefully, I untie the ribbon and lift off the small, shiny lid. Inside is a necklace. I gently pull out the delicate silver chain and hold it up to get a better view. The tiny silver charm twisting there in the makeup lights makes my heart pound.

"What is it?" Chance asks.

"It's an elephant."

Several weeks ago, Rat and I had a conversation on the way to rehearsal. I'd told him about the drama exercise with the elephant.

"Watching the video of the elephant was when it all changed for me," I'd explained.

"Was it male or female?" he'd asked.

"That's not the important part," I'd said. "It was how the elephant moved. How it used its size. That was the impressive part."

"Because if it had a calf that can really make a difference," he'd said.

"I don't know if it had a calf. Again, not the point."

We had pulled into the circle drive of the school and he'd put the car in park. I needed to go to rehearsal, but this was important.

"You don't understand," I'd said. "It's not about the elephant. It's about me."

Rat had leaned over and brushed his lips with mine. Once. Then once again, much longer. My toes had curled up into my shoes, sending the tingle all the way up to the tips of my hair. Elephants, shmelephants. Everything in my brain was suddenly gobbledygook.

"I know it's about you," he'd said slowly, his eyes locked on mine. Suddenly the musical was the last thing on my mind.

"Okay." I'd traced his lips with the tip of my index finger. "Just so you understand."

"I do," he'd said, and kissed me again. Finally, he'd pulled away. "You're going to be late."

I'd opened the car door, suddenly reluctant to leave.

"Was it an Asian elephant or an African elephant?" he'd asked.

"Oh, brother," I'd said, getting out and slamming the door behind me.

I'd still heard him through the closed window, "Because their ears are totally different. The African elephant's ears are much bigger and the tops turn backward."

"Good to know," I'd yelled back over my shoulder.

Now it's opening night and in my hand is a tiny silver elephant charm. I pull the note out of the box. There is no signature. I don't need one.

ELEPHANTS ARE ONE OF THE OLDEST
SYMBOLS OF GOOD LUCK.

Rat's careful all-caps print is instantly recognizable. I quickly slip it on and fasten it around my neck, sliding it down inside the scooped neckline of my white peasant top. I smooth the apron across the long brown skirt of my costume. The contrasting laced bodice fits snug to my body and makes my waist look almost small.

I glance up to see the reflection in the mirror grinning back at me. With her wide grin and dark green eyes sparkling with excitement, the girl in the mirror looks beautiful. The smile . . . *my* smile . . . gets even bigger.

"Places everyone." Ms. DeWise moves quickly through the backstage. "Curtain up in five minutes."

"I'm going," Briella says with a quick hug. "You'll be fantastic," she whispers in my ear.

The bubbles in my stomach rush to my head.

"Break a leg, Ever." Chance grins at me. "Can't wait for our big kiss." He makes kissy noises and pushes his two index fingers together like they're making out.

"Oh, shut up." But I'm laughing.

I walk from the dressing room and take my place stage right. I try to ignore the rustles and hushed whispers going on behind me as opening-night jitters explode backstage. Something about the tension in the air reminds me of waiting to go into surgery — the nerves, the lights, the fear of the unknown. Surgery didn't make everything perfect, but I'm not sorry I went into that operating room.

"Break a leg." Gigi, dressed in the heavy costume of the stepmother, passes on my left with a swish of long skirts.

"You too," I whisper back.

I breathe in the air deeply, filling up my chest. I lift my head and push my shoulders back. The stage is empty in front of me.

It's dimly lit by the swaying brilliance of the waiting spotlights under the thick curtain that separates me from the audience. I hear coughs, muffled laughter, and the squeak of restless bodies in folding theater chairs. A baby cries and is quickly silenced. I feel like my head is lifting off my shoulders. Everything is far, far away.

There is another sound, but I'm the only one who hears it. A whisper. A faint echo. A small, familiar voice.

"You can't . . ."

"You won't . . ."

I know Skinny is here, too, because whether I like it or not, she will always be a part of me. I just don't have to listen to her. Besides, there's too much else in my head, and my heart, to listen to faint echoes. Instead I think of my entrance. My movements. My lines. My music. Those brilliant lights shining on the other side of that curtain tonight will change me forever. I know it. Surgery changed my stomach. Losing weight changed my body. Rat's love changed my heart. But saying good-bye to Skinny changed me most of all. Because Skinny is . . . was . . . me. Now it's her turn to listen. She needs to hear what's going to happen on this stage tonight.

The squeak of the curtain ropes being pulled echoes backstage as the waiting cast takes a collective breath. The sliver of light in the slit of the closed curtain becomes wider and wider. I stand quiet and, in that moment between when I suck the air into my lungs one more time and then let it out again slowly, the pit orchestra begins to play the overture. The audience goes silent. Waiting.

I stare out at the stage. I lift my hand to my throat, feeling the bump of the tiny elephant charm around my neck. It's time.

The trumpets announce the entrance of the chorus. My fellow cast mates push past me and out into the lights. The herald steps up center stage to loudly proclaim that the prince is giving a ball. The chorus begins to sing, and I pick up the prop packages at my feet. Ms. DeWise nods to me from behind the curtain across the stage. My cue.

I won't hide. Or cower. Or apologize. I know there's room for me out there.

I step out into the light.

ACKNOWLEDGMENTS

Gastric bypass surgery was a positive experience for me, but it wasn't a magic wand. I will always struggle with weight and body image issues. This might be your battle, too. Or you might wrestle with negative thoughts that say you're "too stupid" or "too poor" or "too tall" or "too ugly." Don't believe it. You are so much more.

There is a reason why Ever's last name is Davies. My incredible agent, Sarah Davies, completely adopted Ever's story with a passion and enthusiasm that was contagious. Sarah and I not only share a birthday, but we also understand this story in a way that connected us personally and professionally. I am so grateful for her guidance and expertise. Special thanks also to Julia Churchill, Greenhouse UK agent, for her experienced advice and knowledge of the international marketplace.

Thank you, Scholastic! You are my dream publishing company and you have been fantastic. It was love at first sight when

I first opened a Scholastic Book Club flyer as a student. Later, as a teacher and teacher of teachers, there was nothing better than the day the book order arrived in my classroom. Joining the list of esteemed Scholastic authors is a surreal experience, in the best possible way.

My wonderful editor, Aimee Friedman, first and foremost has the heart of a writer. Her fine editorial skills certainly made this a better book, but her understanding of the writing process and the need for positive reinforcement all along the way nurtured me completely. Thanks especially to Scholastic's Debra Dorfman, Ellie Berger, Lori Benton, David Levithan, Abby McAden, and Elizabeth Parisi for their amazing talents and unwavering support. Thanks also to production editor Starr Baer, for the seamless way everything came together. I publicly apologize to my copy editor, Lauren Cecil, for my awful use of commas, capitals, and quotation marks. You're my unsung hero. I so appreciate the skills you have that I obviously don't share.

My deepest appreciation and gratitude also to Stella Paskins and the team at Egmont UK. I'm thrilled to be a part of the new Electric Monkey imprint.

I am so blessed to have found a writers' group that supports me through every aspect of the publishing journey. YAMuses — Bret Ballou, Katy Longshore, Veronica Rossi, and Talia Vance — are amazing. YAH MUSES! Love you, guys! Virtual hugs all around. Love also to longtime writing partners and wonderful friends Kathi Appelt and Debbie

Leland, who never gave up on me. Lorin Oberweger, your insight and skills brought this manuscript to a new level, and I'm so grateful you're part of my writing team. I raise a toast to my crazy happy-hour work group — Derek Decker, Jody Drager, Heidi Frederiksen, Shelley Haddock, Karmen Kelly, Rod Lucero, Sue Lynham, Heidi Propp, Karen Rattenborg, and Cerissa Stevenson. I always feel your cheers and support.

Jay, thanks for your attentive post-op nursing skills, nurturing caretaking, and your continual support of my dream to write and publish a novel. You've appreciated the crazy, and I thank you for that.

Finally, thanks to my family, who always encouraged my creative side. Dad and Marty, I love you. Mom, I miss you every single day.

Don't miss the next unforgettable
novel from Donna Cooner,

CAN'T LOOK AWAY

There's no crying in the spotlight.

Torrey Grey is famous. At least, on the internet. Thousands of
people watch her popular videos on fashion and beauty. But when
Torrey's sister is killed in an accident — maybe because of Torrey
and her videos — Torrey's perfect world implodes.

Now, strangers online are bashing Torrey. And at her new school,
she doesn't know who to trust. Is queen bee Blair only being sweet
because of Torrey's internet infamy? What about Raylene, who is
decidedly unpopular, but seems to accept Torrey for who she is?
And then there's Luis, with his brooding dark eyes, whose family
runs the local funeral home. Torrey finds herself drawn to Luis and
his fascinating stories about *el Día de los Muertos*, the Day of the
Dead.

As the Day of the Dead draws near, Torrey will have to really
look at her own feelings about death, life, and everything in
between. Can she learn to mourn her sister out of the public eye?

Acclaimed author Donna Cooner brings her signature wisdom,
warmth, and insight to this timely story of what grief means in
today's internet age.

TURN THE PAGE FOR A SNEAK PEEK....

I check to make sure the shot is tight, just a close-up of my face without any sign of the boring beige-walled bedroom. I turn on the camera, sit down in the chair, and stare into the lens.

"Hello, Beauty Stars!" I give my signature wave and smile into the camera. "So I wanted to tell you all what I've been up to. . . ." My voice trails off. For some reason, the look of my fingers distracts me.

Sometimes I say I hate the way my fingers look. There's really nothing wrong with them, but you have to hate something about how you look, right? When other girls say, "Oh, I hate my hair. It's so curly," or another one says, "My thighs are huge," then I say, "I just hate my fingers. They are so stubby." I figure why not make the hated body part something that really doesn't count. Lately though, I've been kind of thinking my fingers really are ugly. I stop the recording, watching my fingers carefully. I'll delete that clip. I push RECORD again.

"Hello, Beauty Stars!" *Do the wave again. Don't focus on your fingers.* "I'm so sorry I haven't posted for so long. So many of you have tweeted to ask where I've been lately and I wanted to update you. . . ."

I stop recording, then watch the clip. Even with the extra lamp, the lighting is horrible. And you can make out a sliver of the wall behind me. A hint of the bedroom.

The tour of my room back in Colorado was one of the highest-viewed posts. There were countless comments on my pink walls, vintage pillows, and cute closet-organizing techniques. My subs will note the difference. How am I supposed to explain this? The face reflected in the monitor is like a ghost over the images on screen. My eyes look so tired. And sad. The tears well up and spill silently down my cheeks. It's all too much. I don't know where to start.

I wipe my tears off my face with the back of one hand. The mascara has smeared. This isn't what my fans sign on to watch. They want to see whether I'm wearing purple Toms or gray New Balance sneakers. They want me to tell them whether to buy a MAC 222 crease brush or a MAC 220 blending brush for their Bobbi Brown eye shadow. My vlogs are always supposed to be confident, inspirational, and delightfully personal. Viewers know all about me. They want to be me. It's a big responsibility.